· *Bake-Face* ·

and Other Guava Stories

by *Opal Palmer Adisa*

KELSEY ST. PRESS

A section of "Duppy Get Her" was excerpted in the Summer 1985 issue of *Zyzzyva*. An earlier version of "Widows' Walk" appeared in *San Francisco Stories*.

Bake-Face and Other Guava Stories

by Opal Palmer Adisa

Introduction

by Barbara Christian

KELSEY ST. PRESS   BERKELEY 1986

Bake-Face & Other Guava Stories was set in Palatino by Heyday Books
and was printed in an edition of 2,000 copies by Delta Lithograph
Co. in Los Angeles.

LIBRARY OF CONGRESS CATALOGING IN PUBLICATION DATA

Adisa, Opal Palmer, 1954–
    Bake-face & other guava stories.

        Contents: Bake-face — Duppy get her —
Me man angel — (etc.)
        1. Women—Jamaica—Fiction. I. Title.
PR9265.9.A35B3   1985   813   86-7174

ISBN 0-932716-20-2

Second Edition/May 1987

Published by
Kelsey St. Press
P.O. Box 9235
Berkeley, CA 94709

To Leonie, my sister—a friend with whom I share laughter and tears—and to my girlfriends Pamela, Joan, Rosalind and Marcia, whose history is also rooted in these stories. May the sisters without voices be given microphones.

To Halley
who remembers
the sea

4-14-89

· Contents ·

· *Introduction* ·

Opal Palmer Adisa is a Jamaican woman writer. The four stories she has collected in this volume are about her sisters, contemporary Jamaican women. Not the ones you might see on TV travel ads, who are eternally smiling as they serve you, but women who must struggle to maintain their integrity, as much as their physical survival, in a society plagued for centuries by slavery, colonialism and poverty. These women are descendants of African slaves, and the reality of their lives has been camouflaged by the perennial image the Caribbean evokes for outsiders—an image that merges, paradoxically, paradise and servitude.

But Adisa's women do not see themselves as things created for use. Although constrained by social conditions, they have inner lives that sometimes even they cannot understand, and a sense of a particular way of life to which they can refer. They reach for self-expression in a world which offers them little access to literacy, far less education and self-cultivation, but a world which values the spoken word, an art in which they naturally participate.

In writing about her sisters who still live in the Jamaican countryside, Opal Adisa gives voice to their pleasures, conflicts and feelings as few Jamaican writers before her have done. Her stories are about a plantation worker, a domestic, a village wife, and a fisherman's wife, women who constitute the majority of Jamaican women but who seldom appear as central in even their countrymen's works. Just the existence of this collection, then, is significant, for seldom have we heard the voices of Jamaican rural women who have yet to be directed to the cities, to the metropolises of the world, women who defy our version of who a contemporary woman should be. In refusing to idealize them either as overt rebels or content earth mothers, Adisa attempts to express their complexity.

Not surprisingly, the central character in each of these stories is a mother or a mother-to-be, the one role all Jamaican women are expected to play, whether they live in the town or the country, whether they are middle-class or working-class. Motherhood for these women is the inevitable result of sex, to which they know they have a natural right. Yet each of Adisa's four protagonists relates quite differently to motherhood. Lilly, the domestic in "Duppy Get Her," must have her baby at home, in the land of her mother and mother's mother; the child belongs to her maternal ancestors regardless of where she or the father might be. In contrast, Bake-Face leaves her daughter and husband for part of each year to live with her love Mr. Johnson. Denise MacFarlane, the major character in "Me Man Angel," resents the younger seven of her nine children, for she feels that they "forced themselves on her without giving her time to prepare for them" and that their very existence has distorted her husband's relationship to her. However, in "Widows' Walk," June-Plum enjoys her four children but doesn't want any more, as times are hard. For these four mothers, the experience of motherhood is as varied as the shapes of their bodies, the contours of their personalities. Unlike the smiling nannies' on TV, their attitude towards their children, and therefore themselves, is affected by their bonds with other people, sometimes with their men, often with their own mothers.

In fact, a thread that runs throughout these stories is these women's relationship to *their* mothers and to other women. If they have any telling relationship, either satisfactory or not, it is their sense of their maternal forebears. In "Duppy Get Her" that relationship is central, for Lilly is possessed by her grandmother's call to come home to have her baby. For Bake-Face, the death of her parents at a tender age leaves her uncared for and vulnerable to the harsh male world. The lack of a mother will affect the way her personality develops. In contrast, the sweet and prickly June-Plum remembers her mother with fondness.

Along with their mothers, other women provide solace, advice, care, sometimes grief, to these women. It is the strong women's community of the plantation which helps Bake-Face to feel more at ease with herself; still, it is other women who cause her confusion and whom she tries to understand. In "Widows' Walk," the complexity of a woman's relationship with herself is heightened, for it is Yemoja, the female West African loa of the ocean still revered by New World blacks, whom June-Plum must come to know. June-Plum's growing understanding of the goddess Yemoja is as much the major theme of this story as the woman's wait for her fisherman husband.

The ties between these women and the men they love or marry are also critical to these stories. As for women throughout the world who live in societies where survival is a struggle, cooperation between the sexes or the lack of it can gravely affect the quality of life. What is important to me is that Adisa presents these relationships from the women's point of view, one that is often missing in Caribbean literature. As a result, we come to feel these women's desires and fears, their sensuality, their power or lack of it. Such a point of view, however, cannot be adequately portrayed except through these women's language, for it is their language that reveals their deeper values and their sense of themselves.

Adisa captures the nuances of Jamaican English derived from African languages, 17th century British English and the specific experience of Jamaican life as only a native Jamaican can. For an American audience, the language of these Jamaican women may, at first, be hard to hear. But because of Adisa's use of the inherently sensual quality of these women's speech, we feel, and then begin to hear, the nuances of their speech patterns. Rooted in the Jamaican countryside, the atonal speech of her characters is inextricably a part of flamboyant Nature, its exuberance of color, its fecundity. Although linked to other Caribbean peoples' transformation of British English, Adisa's Jamaican English is as different from the great Barbadian American writer Paule Marshall's language as Barbados is from Jamaica. Readers would make a mistake if they equated the different forms of English in the Caribbean and would miss the very nuances that give Adisa's stories so much of their unique quality. In remaining true to these nuances, Adisa gives these women their proper sound, that peculiar blending of "the King's English" and their everyday experiences as Jamaican women. So the constancy of the sun, the alluring rhythm of the ocean, and the burst of vivid color in the landscape are the natural stuff of metaphor for them. It is through these natural images that they give form to their thoughts, feelings, insights—their particular feminine experiences.

When I was a girl growing up in the Caribbean, I was amazed by the verbal skill of even the most lowly market women. Like Paule Marshall, I was stunned by these "talking women," among whom were my mother and aunts. In spite of my greedy consumption of books, I never met one such woman in any book. And I was told by my teachers that it was quite clear that these women's language (my language as well) was not even a language, since it never appeared in print. In other words, we were as discredited as our language.

Opal Palmer Adisa, and writers like her who give their sisters' voices a written expression, may reverse that concept and help us to achieve the understanding and respect we have always deserved. These writers, as well, are helping to recreate the English language for all of us.

Barbara Christian

Barbara Christian is Associate Professor of Afro-American Studies at the University of California at Berkeley. She is the author of *Black Feminist Criticism: Perspectives on Black Women Writers*, Pergamon Press (1985), *Black Women Novelists: the Development of A Tradition 1892–1976*, Greenwood Press (1980), and *Teaching Guide to Black Foremothers*, Feminist Press (1980). *Black Women Novelists*, the first book on this subject, won the Before Columbus American Book Award in 1983. Her essays on black women writers have appeared in many literary and academic journals.

· *Bake-Face* ·

THE blood-red petals of the flamboyant tree cover the ground like a dropt flag over a coffin. By the end of the day the sun will have sucked the petals, leaving them shrivelled, to be blown by the wind or swept away by children. Already, as the day wears on, the petals take on the appearance of dried blood on a piece of white cloth. To the barefoot, the ground is an oven, so that all things in the environment seem to be conspiring to close another chapter on this bivouac.

Sitting with eyes closed and her back supported by the coconut-tree trunk, Bake-Face puffs on her pipe, inhaling the tobacco aroma, her face as smooth and wrinkle-free as a newly made bed. People pass her by with the same indifference that they show to the leaves that they tread upon in the yard of Bruk-up House. From where she sits, she can see the other women in their kitchens, the traffic to and from the bathrooms, the children at play and some of the movements in the lane in front of the house.

Apart from a few forming wrinkles, Bake-Face's body could pass for that of a young girl's. Her knees are pulled up to her chest, her slender legs shining from coconut oil; her long, thick black plaits glow under the sun and her high cheek-bones suggest an intrinsic beauty that is fading and mournful from lack of recognition. Her cheeks are hollow.

Noman Estate, a sugar plantation, is a ghost town for seven months of the year while the canes grow and ripen. Then, it rises like bread bursting in the middle for the remainder of the year when the seasonal workers return with their muscle-power, gossip, superstitions and loud carousing. The beginning of the crop season is as tense as the ending, but the latter is wrought with

3

more anxiety, as it marks the end of the manna period. Food, money and work are always dubious, and those who have not been frugal enough to put away a few pennies during the season know that worrying about employment and ban belly are part of the ritual of crop-over.

The workers live in large tenement dwellings erected close to the factory. Bruk-up, the largest of these houses, is the temporary home of the more skilled workers and their families. It is a spacious, twelve-room building two stories high with the largest apartments downstairs reserved for the supervisors.

All around Bake-Face children play, kicking up dirt with their bare feet. The sun is its usual hot, gallant self, but a cool wind blows from the fields. The clothes on the many lines flap noisily about, as if clapping hands while singing—apart together, apart together. Two green lizards on the barbed wire fence fight over a fly. A mongoose darts into the nearby bushes. Miss Kelly's maid across the fence is still washing since yesterday by the stand-pipe in the middle of her yard which provides running water. Her hands go squish-squish as she rubs the clothes against her rough palms. Bake-Face savors all these activities, which are not new, but which she will leave in three days when she returns to her own man, her child and her own house. Yet these sights are what she lives for; they hold memories—some burnt molasses, bitter and scalding to the tongue, others thick cane juice, frothy and sweet—of her and Mr. Johnson. Three more days, and she and Mr. Johnson will part, not meeting again until next year when the canes are ripe and ready for cutting.

How long has it been now? Five years since she and Mr. Johnson have been carrying on, and as usual, before they part, she will make blue-drawers, his favorite cakes stained blue with banana leaves, so that he will have some to take to his real home, a place not as sweet as this sugar estate or her blue-drawers, but a home nonetheless, where she is not welcome. "Frank Johnson!" The name issues from Bake-Face's mouth like a hot breath of air. A contemptuous snicker and shaking of her head from side to side accompany this journey back into the past.

Pauline, her first and only child, was four months old when Bake-Face first met Mr. Johnson. "Pauline was burnin' up wid feva. Me did fraid God was gwane tek me one little picknie to punish me fah me silence." Bake-Face had wrapped up her child and travelled the twenty-five miles to the nearest hospital, which was always a pot with too much food in it. She sat on the hard wooden bench with other mothers like herself, old groaning men and women with sores, young men with hands and feet and limbs sliced away by a slip from their machetes or bottle wounds from lack of shoes, and other women with pains from too much work, too much living, too much giving birth, too much not being able to find enough. Bake-Face's heart was heavy and sweat covered her body as she sat waiting, not patiently, but having no choice, to see one of the two doctors who attended to hundreds of people weekly, treating simple cuts, sores, flu, toothaches, pregnancy, delivery, whatever ailed the masses of people like herself who had no income or means to seek private doctors. Her eyes took in those who talked among themselves to keep their spirits high.

It was then that she noticed one other, silent like herself, but whose eyes took in all the details. He was a big brown man who cradled a child about five years old close to his chest. She looked from the child to the man and their eyes locked, and very plainly reflected in his hazel eyes was her sorrow, as plain on his face as the beady perspiration that she wiped occasionally from her face with the palm of her hand and her dress-tail. "Ah couldn't tek me eyes off im; den Pauline start to bawl an me push me titty inna er mout." Then Frank Johnson, not being sure of himself but compelled by a desire he hadn't felt in too many years, reached out his hand and touched her face, running it up and down her cheeks, pressing her high cheek bones, testing the strength of her neck and her collar bone, fondling her face as if it were a piece of wood he had carved. And she drank in his touch hungrily, like the child who was

5

suckling on her breast, so he decided right there that he would have her, not as an exploit, but because she was a frail chicken left to fend for corn with the haggard fowls. They called his name then and he took his daughter in to see the nurse. Afterward he waited two-and-a-half hours until Bake-Face saw the doctor and got the medicine for her puny-looking child. Sensing that she was without transportation, he offered her a ride in his old jeep.

They rode in silence, and as he was full of his feelings, his hands would not reach out to her. She sat there, her eyes hard and blank like cardboard, waiting for some destiny to be stamped upon her. They were by her gate and no commitment had been sealed; he saw the square-shaped, brown-painted house sitting fifteen yards in from the gate, and he knew she didn't live there but somewhere inside herself, and that decided him: "Ah will be in town nex week dis same time; meet me ten o'clock by de post office." She blinked, mumbled thanks, and went through the gate. A tired hound barked from the side of the house. He turned the jeep around. Feeling as if his heart were in his palms, he drove home with much difficulty.

The remainder of the week that ushered in their meeting crawled by—led by an ant, Bake-Face was certain. No food would go past her throat and her stomach pressed against her back. She looked through her few belongings and found nothing with color, but they met, her hair greased, her nails clean and her eyes an unsure dance. Very little was said between them; they weren't talkers, but they drove around all day, stopping by the sea, where she lifted up her skirt and exposed her bamboo legs, and he dreamed of feeling them about him. So, they parted with only a pocket full of words, but that was enough, because two months later, having only met him three times excluding the day at the hospital, Bake-Face boarded a train to join Frank Johnson at Noman Estate. She left Pauline, her husband Ezra, and his four sons with Cutie, Ezra's sixteen-year-old cousin who only the week before had been put out by her parents for repeatedly lifting up her skirt for boys.

On the train to join Frank Johnson, Bake-Face reflected on her life. She did care for Ezra, her husband and father of her only child. Ezra had certainly saved her from Bellview, the island's insane asylum; he had been good to her all the eleven years after he took her in, an orphan child abused by aunts who because they could not protect her or defend themselves, out of jealousy and frustration accused her of spreading her legs for her uncles. She had been crazy with loneliness which ate at her body, making her look like a frail vine. There were cousins who also knew that she did not know how to protest or seek revenge; and there were others who found no one else to vent their hostilities on, and so abused her. Then, one day, Ezra walked in: he sat watching as she brought him and her uncle a cool glass of lemonade, and he watched her uncle pinch her breast, his chuckling like water going down the sewer.

Throughout the two days he stayed at her uncle's house, he saw the man's wife hit her in the face and abuse her with foul words. He noted the children ordering her about like a mule, yet she held her back stiff throughout, her eyes blank. Just before Ezra left, he approached her: "Ah ave four bwoy dem; dem is good. Las yam season ah put me wife in de ground. Ah need someone fi help wid de house; yuh will get food, shelter an change, no abuse." And so she had packed up her three dresses, her other meager items, and left without any good-bye or backward glance.

And he was a man of his word. He had never shouted at her or raised his hand to bruise her body. He cared for her in his clumsy way: he allowed her the same freedom as he did his sons. He had kept her in his house for three months before marrying her, and though they slept in the same room, in the same bed, he never once, before the pastor mumbled some words at them, touched her. This decided Bake-Face that he was a fisherman like Peter in the Bible. True, he only went fishing occasionally, but he was strong and kind to her like the story she had heard of Jesus' first disciple.

The marriage was a great displeasure to the community—that the most eligible of their village had taken unto himself a complete stranger who hardly spoke to anyone and who looked like an emaciated dog. But Ezra Joshua Beard kept right on with Bake Face, and even flogged his sons when they disrespected her. He was generous to her, too, giving her change separate from the house money and even buying her clothes. Now she had a dozen dresses, so she owed him something for his kindness, but perhaps not all of her life. She needed to live a little bit, and Frank Johnson was the first and only man who made her heart race. She discovered that laughter found her and she could cry, something which had been alien to her before. She cried without fearing that the ground would open up and take her in.

Not once did Bake-Face have second thoughts or feel any regrets about going off, even under the gashing tongues of the village. She was for the first time excitedly curious about someone, and wanted to understand this new sensation. She did not know . . . after all these years, *still* she isn't sure why she and Mr. Johnson were brought together, only that they were, and together, they supplied a deficiency in each other. But Bake-Face's thoughts on the train that first time to meet her man five years ago were mostly those of a schoolgirl on her first trip from home. The many new sights made her feel like a rainbow floating on air.

Time has once again galloped off, except this time her heart is banging against her chest and her head is a Pocamania revival meeting. She knows that the days before her departure should be special—as sweet as the cakes she is going to bake—yet she also knows that she will only speak to Mr. Johnson when necessary. She will probably pull her tiny body up close to the wall, shrugging away his hands. Already the impending separation and the memories of their love are painful. It is always the same before they part: his touch, their loving, is like burning paper—only the black ash which stains everything remains. This is the space she needs before returning to Ezra and a home where the trees don't bloom or bear fruits (all male trees) and before Johnson returns to a wife, who from his stories, is larger than the flamboyant tree and much sturdier, too.

"Frank Johnson"—again it escapes her lips. Bake-Face shakes her head. "Ah always calls im Missa Johnson like eberyone else. Ah suppose it cause of that first time." He didn't meet her like he said he would; he was working and sent someone else. It was Ernest, and during the eight-mile ride from the train to Bruk-up House, Ernest kept referring to Mr. Johnson as Mr. Johnson this and Mr. Johnson that. It was then she realized that she had never before called him anything because they were not that intimate, and she was still thinking about what to call him when she arrived at Bruk-up House. Ernest introduced her to Joyce, who led her to Mr. Johnson's room. So she decided then to call him Mr. Johnson, because the name obviously commanded respect.

The breeze and the dirt wane and whine. Bake-Face closes her eyes. A blossom falls on her head; her hand reaches up to brush it away, but she leaves it, wearing it like a crown. A chicken lays an egg, then cackles. The red peel-neck rooster pursues it. Bake-Face picks up a stone, throwing it playfully at the rooster. One of Brownie's puppies, realizing its individuality, wanders away. Bake-Face motions to the pup, snapping her fingers and repeating, "Come, puppy, puppy." It tentatively comes up and frisks her skirt; she places it on her lap, rubbing its back absent-mindedly.

Richard, wearing only pants and carrying a towel, rag and soap in his hands, gallops down the stairs. He is a pot-boiler living in one of the upstairs rooms with Carol. They share the house with seven single men and three families who leave their permanent homes every year during crop season to travel to Noman Estate and live in Bruk-up House. Members of a seasonal family, they pick up their lives from where they left off the previous crop season. Richard stops in front of Bake-Face.

"Wha appen, Bake-Face? Tree days and we gone again like de dust we sweep way from in front we step ebery marnin. Me pan de two-to-ten shift, but yuh fi save some blue-drawers fi me."

Bake-Face's eyes rest on Richard's naked torso before advancing to his hairy chest, wide shoulders and handsome, boyish face with the smile of a ginal, a suave charmer. She smiles, revealing two missing teeth knocked out by an uncle as he forced himself on her. She smacks her lips. When Bake-Face speaks, her voice is flat. Her pace is slow and even—irritating, yet appealing. "Richard, de mount of drawers yuh pull off ooman me would tink yuh wouldn't wan nuh more fi eat."

Richard frowns at Bake-Face before emitting a gargling kind of laughter. He likes Bake-Face bad. Sure, he has women, but none of them wear a ring for him. With Bake-Face, it is a different matter. Just now, her second finger on her left hand flaunted the ring of a husband—not Mr. Johnson. But did that prevent her from leaving her husband's house for five months each year for the past five years, so that she could live with and take care of Mr. Johnson, married himself to someone else and with a family of his own? No, he will keep his women, but Bake-Face and Mr. Johnson should decide. How much longer do they think they can carry on this affair? Richard shakes his head, then turns to take his shower, leaving behind his perceptions of Bake-Face.

Although one cannot tell from looking at Bake-Face (her face is an empty sheet of paper), she is quite adept at reading people's minds, and Richard's thoughts are like a curse. No one understands about her and Mr. Johnson. No. No one knows where the shoe pinches but he who wears it. If it weren't for the ripening cane, this estate, this very house, her and Mr. Johnson's lives would be the sadness of a mother whose child died.

Up until six years ago, her life was a grave dug too early—there was no body or coffin to put in it, but that did not prevent the rain from falling, filling in the grave, taking a piece of her spirit with it. Then, Frank Johnson came along and rescued her from the drudgery of Ezra. Ezra knew where she went every year, from the very first time, but he said nothing as long as she found some other woman to do all her chores in her absence, and when she returned, she allowed him to release himself. It was good luck that he infrequently needed sexual release. He was often forceful in much the same way as he dealt with his farm, which thrived relentlessly. Bake-Face withstood his occasional arousal, thankful that she wasn't the soil he went out to deal with buoyantly every morning.

Bake-Face travels further and feels her stomach go flip-flop as she remembers the events leading up to her daughter's birth. She was as surprised as was the village when Pauline came, having long given up hope of having a child. The first time her uncle raped her, she was twelve and already seeing blood, so she feared all month, but nothing happened and he kept on, and others took their cue from him and used her like the soil, but her stomach still remained close to her back. So naturally, after seven years of living with Ezra and nothing happening, the village had given up on her, had long ceased to jeer at Ezra about the mule he had picked up and made his wife.

She was five months pregnant before she realized that she was with child. She was never sick a day during the entire pregnancy and her dresses still fit her, except they were a little tight around the waist. Pauline was born in the dirt one afternoon as Bake-Face stooped by her kitchen picking sorrel, a healthy six-pound child with a thick head of hair and Ezra's stern forehead. The village came out and made merry. Ezra killed a goat and a hog, and people came and rested their hands on her shoulder. Some women even offered advice, and the festivity kept on for three days, the grandpa of the village remarking that it was better than any marriage or funeral he had ever attended.

11

Bake-Face sniffles, using the back of her hand to wipe away the tears that run down her cheeks. The earth doesn't even tremble, though her chest heaves. She is a dying leaf, and the people of Bruk-up yard walk blindly by as she breaks from the stem of the branch and falls. The puppy snuggles in the folds of Bake-Face's skirt, disturbed by her heaving. She picks it up to her face, staring into its watery eyes, remembering how at birth its eyes were tightly closed and it kept close to its mother, nestling under her stomach, hearing only her protective growl.

She hears the voices of the children at play, their laughter and bickering harmonious. The breeze blows the dirt about, the children oblivious of it in their matted hair. Once again her daughter appears in her eyes, a vine like her, but sturdy and carefree, happy when Bake-Face is there but seemingly just as happy in her absence. "Ah suppose is cause me did lef er wen she was suh young," Bake-Face mumbles.

Richard emerges from the shower, his back wet, with soap on his hair above his right ear. As he passes by Bake-Face, he is touched by her sadness. Muttering, Richard climbs the stairs: "Lawd, ooman dem did wicked to demself sah. Dem always fall in love an shed tears. Jus spoil a good ting. Same ting wid Shirley an Carol; de both a dem a fight ova me like me is collection plate. Cho! Ooman!" Richard shakes his head and mounts another step. He pauses, then adds, "Bake-Face keep special feelins, dough, cho!"

Wincing, Bake-Face glances at the sun, which is no longer fierce. Sometimes it appears to her to emit a sound like the bleating of sheep. She slides the puppy from her lap: "Go fin yuh muma, puppy—me man gwane be home soon an me nuh put pot pan de fire yet." The puppy lingers. Bake-Face gives it a slight push with her foot. Looking down at it with eyes muddy like the river after a storm, Bake-Face announces: "Puppy, ah gwane tek yuh home wid me fah Pauline; she will like yuh bad." But the puppy walks away with a dejected wag of its tail.

Gracefully, Bake-Face pulls herself up, brushing

off the back of her dress. She holds her back erect—
statuesque; only her dress, blown by the breeze, does
a hulahoop dance.

She walks to the kitchen, a building like the bathroom, about twenty yards from the main house. Inside
the kitchen, Bake-Face lowers her nose inside the pot
to smell the meat she seasoned earlier this morning.
She smacks her lips and pours oil in the Dutch pot
after lighting the stove. Fumbling through her cupboard, she tries to find something else that will please
Mr. Johnson: "Ah gwane be happy dese las few days,"
she vows. "Me a guh look inna Johnson eye an smile,"
Bake-Face resolves, finding three fingers of green
banana and a pack of white rice.

A voice from the side of Bruk-up House asks:
"Bake-Face, whe yuh deh?"

"Ah in ere. Who dat?"

"Is me, Bake-Face, Ernest."

"Mass Ernest, long time nuh see." She smiles
and puts one hand akimbo. Ernest is Johnson's best
friend, so she likes him. Besides, he is always polite
to her and often treats her with the respect normally
reserved for older women. She stands in her kitchen
doorway watching Ernest approach: "Yuh come see if
me mek any blue-drawers yet? Nuh worry—me always
tek yours out first, afta me put way Johnson portion."

Ernest's brown, smooth, sweaty face breaks into
a smile. Once again, he sizes up Bake-Face: "She is
nice ooman an cook sweet an all dat, but she nuh me
type—too mawga. Me like me ooman dem fat—plenty
ass and breast, somtin to hold on pan. Me nuh know
wha Johnson see in er part from er cookin. She mawga
bad. Johnson could get some a de nicest ooman dem
tuh. Eh, afta all, im is supervisor of all de pot-boiler
dem, plus im good lookin and ave strong body, an is
decent person, tuh." Ernest shakes his head. He is
aware that Bake-Face is staring at him intently: "Yuh
alrite, Ernest?" she inquires.

"Me jus a come from de factory," he reports.
"Johnson seh fih tell yuh im a do double shift. Im won
come ome fore ten."

Bake-Face pulls in her cheeks and utters from deep within her throat a sound like a pickaxe hitting stones. Ernest shifts his weight.

A ganuh of about eight carriages rolls by loaded down with cane being transported to the factory. Ernest hears some of the cane fall off, and as usual, the wheels of the tractor drive over the cane, crushing out all the sap. So he becomes a piece of cane in front of Bake-Face. Yet her own rupture is evident, making her at once cane and tractors' wheels.

Bake-Face recalls five years ago, a Thursday evening when she arrived at Bruk-up House and Noman Estate. All the tenants seemed so intimate; their voices resounded like the cacophony of insects at night. The next day, Joyce befriended her, and told her why the house was called "Bruk-up." Apparently, it was the cause of many broken relationships. She didn't learn any of the details then, because her mind was on herself and Mr. Johnson. Although they had not spoken, she knew he had a wife and at least one child. He knew about her likewise. She wasn't accustomed to people talking to her and telling her about their lives, but she hoped that Johnson would tell her something about himself. She felt the need to tell him about her life although she and Ezra had not exchanged more than a dozen sentences about each other. They knew through seeing, and what the eyes did not see, the lips did not reveal. That Thursday night, if she had been a woman with hopes and expectations, she would have been angry and disappointed, because Johnson not only did not meet her at the train, he did not come home that night. There was some problem at the factory, and he worked all through the night until ten o'clock the next morning. When he came home, all he said to her before falling off to sleep was: "De train ride de alrite?" She only had a chance to nod her head, because the next thing she knew he was snoring. Not knowing what to do with herself, she had wandered outside and sat by the mango tree, and that was where Joyce had joined her, pointing out all the people and introducing her to the other women and their children, and showing Bake-Face her kitchen.

Ernest clears his throat. Bake-Face looks through him. He hears the voices of two women cane-cutters and feels rescued. Their robust, inviting voices, free like the wind, reach out to him; he envisions their large behinds, rumbling like waves of cane after sunset. The yearning to firmly grip buttocks overcomes him. The musk smell of the cane and sweat fills his nostrils as he relives the many afternoon rest periods when he rolled around the fields with one of these women; his penis hardens and he rubs it, forgetting Bake-Face, who has now turned her back on him anyway.

Two days passed before she and Johnson sat down to speak. He had worked until ten, and she had not eaten, waiting until he came. Then she took their dinner on a tray and laid the table. The night was hot, and the aroma of rum hung in the air as the cane-fields burned. It was then she learned that they burnt the fields to make cutting the cane easier for the men and women. After they ate in silence and as she was clearing the table, Johnson caught hold of her wrist and pulled her onto his lap. He looked at her face as if searching for something; then, he kissed her eyes and her cheeks and her entire face. He was so gentle that before she could control herself, tears swelled big and she held him around the neck and cried because he was the first man who had loved her, wanting her for something more than a hole to release himself in. She poured all the years of pain and anguish from her heart. He held her close to his chest, caressed her hands, ran his hand through her hair, and she loved him. But then she felt so naked that for almost a month she could not bear to look in his face. In the midst of others, if he looked at her, she turned inward and the words from her mouth sounded like babbling.

From somewhere in the distance, Bake-Face hears her name. She turns and sees Ernest still standing there. Hearing the capricious voices trailing off like a loose kite taken by the wind, Ernest speaks, racing against an invisible clock: "Bake-Face, ah will see yuh. Memba, now, save some blue-drawers fah me. An, oh,

Johnson seh im will try reach ome fore ten." He trots off and Bake-Face shakes her head, waving her hand after Ernest as if he were a fly circling around her face that she wanted to brush away. Ernest runs through the short cut, leaving Bake-Face sadder than ever

The shaggy puppy, light brown like its mother, rubs its body against Bake-Face's foot. She looks down at it, sucking in her cheeks, her expression giving her face a skeletal look. Her eyes stare at the hedges of love-bush, the seeds of which Carol scattered a few months ago when asking for Richard's love. Seeing how it has spread in abundant wildness, Bake-Face snickers. Everyone knows Richard has at least one other woman, Shirley, who just dropped picknie for him.

She leans against the door post of her kitchen, the puppy in her arm. She rubs its back, and it yawns lazily. On the horizon, the sun is an orange-pink taffeta, but the air is stale like a room closed for the season. She notes that the grass needs cutting. As is usual just before the crop comes to an end, the yard is left uncared for. Yet the vegetable beds which the women tend are lush with callalloo, cabbage, tomato, chocho, and along one side of the yard, gungu peas. The sounds of women banging pots and pans, preparing meals for their men and children, return Bake-Face to the present. "Nuh need hurry. Johnson nuh come ome any time soon." Her eyes turn to the sky: the clouds are on the warpath, grey and threatening. Carol greets her as she bends to pick a bunch of callalloo. Bake-Face observes her, wondering if she has told Richard that she is with his child. Already her back is pressed inward to accommodate her stomach, which is swollen outward.

Just like women, reflects Bake-Face, giving when they shouldn't and hoping when all hopes have been buried. Why do they think they are so powerful, so capable of changing and molding? Why do they allow men to enter, to show them spit and sometimes fists, and still cook for them without putting piss in the food and without filling the beds with daggers instead of warmth? Why do men act so mighty, never noticing their own weakness, dismissing their rape, wearing women's love like shirts, ejecting children like shit, showing their backs as if they do not bleed too? She knows that they do, other women know that they do, but men don't know, because they don't have to shop once a month for pads to catch a part of themselves from spilling onto the earth. Even Johnson sometimes forgets that he bleeds. He is tender, but beyond that there is his shell. That first night they were together, he had pulled out her soul with his kisses, but it was not until the second crop season that she had learned what his life was like at home with his wife and children.

Frank Johnson is a big man, six feet even with broad chest and skin like yam, wavy hair and a perfect set of teeth. He isn't a talker; he had jokingly told Bake-Face that his wife took his tongue away with her nagging, and perhaps she also took his smile, because he rarely does. But when he does, his face seems boyish and his lips curl up. He told Bake-Face that he liked her because her eyes were like the ocean, and he said her skin looked like varnished coconut-shell and felt even better, and that she was a stick that he could enfold.

That second crop season was the most he had ever spoken, although they lay for many hours beside each other. She was afraid that he would think her like his wife, so she swallowed her words, which some-times choked her. He never seemed to notice her silence, so she had decided that that was another thing she would learn to live with. Now she doesn't want to live with it any more; it is stifling her and there is no alternative. To ask for more than a season would be suicide; part of the pleasure was that it was merely temporary. Her spirit is involved, but it has not wings with which to fly. Her chest heaves, but her eyes are dry. Her arms reach up, resting on her head, her hands clutch her elbows, but no tears fall. The orange-pink taffeta sky turns mauve, and the sun has gone some-where else. The mosquitoes and sand flies are being festive.

Ezra is probably eating his supper, and her Pauline is most likely at the back steps with the boys and other children swapping stories, and if what Johnson said is true, Mrs. Rebecca Johnson, an amazon of no small order, is putting food on the table for her seven children and Joseph, Mrs. Johnson's other husband—the man who sleeps on Mr. Johnson's side of the bed for the five months he is away.

Rebecca Johnson is a woman of forty like her husband, but she looks all the years of her age. She has borne thirteen children in all. Three died at birth, one drowned when he was two years old and the older two she gave to her brother in America who had no children. She is from a large family—her mother had seventeen. All of them lived and learned to survive with fists and mouth. She is a woman men call handsome, her skin the color of earth, her hair thick, a big-boned body equal to the strength of any man except that she is curved and when she walks, her hips roll and her feet dance on the soil. That was what caught Johnson's eyes, her movement. The first time, at nineteen, when they rolled around in the bush, they made child, and when she came to tell him, her fists ready for a fight, he did right by her without any protest. The first years were pleasant enough, but Rebecca was not a patient woman, and her needs were plenty. Johnson was a dedicated family man who worked hard and was often not up to the task at night. Rebecca did not feel she should suffer for his inability, so she sought and found sugar somewhere else. When Johnson found out, it was fist for fist that night, and next morning they were both bruised. From then on Rebecca controlled herself and as she birthed another child, her tongue got looser until it became disconnected from her face and Johnson sealed his ears with cotton. For fourteen years he tucked his tail between his legs, loving Rebecca when he could and ignoring her as much as she permitted. He was happy to be by himself during the cane season; then he met Bake-Face and he wanted more. Leaving Rebecca was never more than an idea because she wouldn't permit him, and Bake-Face was satisfied with the arrangement, too.

"Eheh!" Bake-Face trembles. It was the third crop season that she met Mrs. Johnson. She wasn't fearful when the big woman walked into Bruk-up yard and declared, as loud as the whistle which sounded to announce the time, that she was Mrs. Johnson, wife of Frank Johnson, and demanded to know who it was that was keeping her husband's clothes clean for her. Bake-Face was sitting over a tub of clothes at the time and was not mortified. Years of abuse had prepared her for the encounter. For a moment her hands had rested idly; then they continued scrubbing. Rebecca Johnson had stood over her smiling, all two hundred and fifty pounds of her, her shadow that of a giant, and laughed. Then in that same loud manner, which drew a crowd, she said: "So yuh is Bake-Face. Eh suh wha a way yuh did mawga. Me neba know that Johnson like mawga ooman. But ah suppose im need a rest fi deal wi me." She burst into thunderous laughter, her hands akimbo. Bake-Face didn't remember much what else she said, because she closed her ears thereafter. She went inside herself, and when she came back out, the woman was gone. The other women, children, dogs, pigeons, and the few men who were home then had gone back to their chores, partially happy but disappointed that no fight had taken place.

The puppy in Bake-Face's arms yelps and wiggles. She lets it down gently. Evening has wrapped itself around like a snake. Closing her kitchen door, she walks to the mango tree—her shrine.

Children are ushered by their mothers to go and wash their feet and make ready for bed. Their eyes accuse, still wanting to play, but they obey, although an occasional under-breath grumble can be heard. People in Bruk-up yard move back and forth. "Bake-Face, yuh alrite?" reaches her many times. Each time she nods an affirmative, annoyed by the seemingly endless activity, all the time someone coming and going, making Bruk-up a thoroughfare.

She rubs her eyes. It will be at least three more hours before Johnson comes home. "Karen!" She calls to one of the children to fetch her pipe from her room. The child hastily does as bid. Women go to their rooms with their men's food neatly covered on trays. Small children are fed and sent to bed while the older ones sit by the side of the house telling stories and solving riddles.

Bake-Face pulls on her pipe. Men come home, eat, go to sleep. Some leave for bars or other backyards, to cards and domino games. Some of the women sit with the children and teach them their history; others mend and sew. The younger ones gather on the upstairs veranda, sharing the details of their men's loving as well as their fears and longings.

Tonight, Bake-Face doesn't feel like being a part of any group. She looks on, half listening, making connections. Here she is, like all the other women who live in Bruk-up House: they love these men, sometimes taking abuse from them, and none of them are married to any of them, even though some have taken their men's names. In fact, she and Mr. Johnson are the only ones who separated after the crop season ended. The other families remained together, except for Richard and Paul, who have no special women. But perhaps now that Carol is with child and spent the last three crop seasons with Richard, he will stay with her, even though there are four other women who bore him children. Bake-Face sighs. "Poo Carol, she did love like a damn fool." Bake-Face coughs. Today her life is a picture-show that she must look at.

The incident that occurred a month ago is painful gas to be belched. "Dat why Jennifa did guh off like dat; livin in limbo. Avin a husband but nuh name." Bake-Face shakes her head, a slow, heavy movement; each subtle jerk of her body is a whisper of frustration and futility.

Exactly one month and three days ago, Bruk-up yard had the biggest contention in its history. No blood was shed and no physical fight took place, but that is not why it was significant. It was important because the conflict was internal and intimate. Generally speaking, the women and men, but the women in particular, lived and had always lived harmoniously with each other, sharing their vegetables, correcting each other's children, even giving them a lick if the occasion demanded it, advising and consoling each other before Jennifer's attack.

It was another regular stew-peas and rice Wednesday afternoon that Jennifer, Peter's woman and mother of his three children, sat by the mango tree, shelling gungu peas. Jennifer's objective was to cook rice and peas and chicken (Sunday dinner) for Peter this Wednesday evening, since rumor had it that he was sleeping with Maud, the whore of Noman Estate who lived in the barracks with her eight children, all ranging from one to ten, all from eight different men. Maud's reputation was public news. Also public was her inability to keep any man beyond the crop season. She was quite adept at seducing, but failed when it came to retaining. At every end of the season, the men crawled like beaten dogs back to their respective women, begging to be taken back, leaving Maud to fend for herself. But that never stopped Maud, because she always managed to get healthier and fatter after each child. She would come around at the beginning of crop season, swinging her large ass, which looked like a mountain moving of its own accord, before the faces of the men, promising a river of sweetness.

Knowing this, it was understandable that Jennifer was quite frustrated. For the last two weeks, Peter was out until early morning every night, even when he was not on the graveyard shift. Jennifer was not a woman to accept rumors without first testing them. So she took extra pains to oil her body, to fix her hair; she used every opportunity she had, which lately was very little, to rub her body against Peter's. Still she could not arouse him, and that was never a problem before, as they were active lovers. All her efforts having failed, Jennifer accepted rumor as fact. She wasn't hurt simply because Peter was sleeping with Maud; it was because Maud, in a greedy and unfriendly manner, was taking *all* of Peter's strength.

All these thoughts went through Jennifer's head

21

as she sat shelling peas to cook a sweet Sunday dinner for Peter, hoping that Maud would not induce him to eat from her (lest she put something in his food to bind him). It was then that Bake-Face came and sat beside her, sympathizing with her sorrow. With no malice intended, but rather a hope to make light of Jennifer's predicament, Bake-Face jested: "Jennifer, gal, ah see yuh a cook a Sunday dinna fi bind yuh man."

Bake-Face's words declared Jennifer's plans. Instantly, the latter's face grew beady with sweat, her tongue tasted bitter, her head darted around like a mouse smelling a cat. She was on her feet: "Wha it to yuh wha me do wid me man?" She puffed into Bake-Face's face, her words reeling as if rehearsed. "Yuh see me ave husband who me lef a yard an come trow meself pan oda ooman man? Yuh see me leabe me picknie dem a yard fah oda ooman tek care of? Fi me picknie dem always wid me an a de same man me did live wid did fada dem. Me nuh nuh whore like de Maud. She ave me man an me wan im; me will ave im, tuh. Ooman, guh a yuh yard, guh look bout yuh man an picknie an stay out me business." Jennifer stopped, her hands rolled for a fight.

When the commotion started, the other women left off their chores, wiping their hands on their skirt hems, and gathered around Jennifer and Bake-Face. Several times Joyce, the peacemaker of Bruk-up House and Bake-Face's best friend, had tried to butt in using reason, but Jennifer wouldn't hear any of it. The women stared at her with their heads hanging; they shared her sorrow, but could not condone her attack. Bake-Face was not one to interfere or to provoke anyone. Jennifer was out of line. The women stood, grabbing Jennifer with their silence; she felt defeated. All she saw was Maud with her man—Maud, who was as big as the whole outdoors, laughing at her.

Throughout the entire outrage, Bake-Face sat mute, feeling like a discarded shirt fallen in mud. Jennifer's bosom heaved convulsively, her mouth frothed. Grabbing her basin of peas, she fled into her kitchen, peas flying all over the ground, food for the unconcerned chickens, who immediately fought over the grains.

The women put their hands on their heads. Truly, it was as if their mothers were dead: they marked time with their feet, went and covered their pots loudly, and shouted at their children to go and take pennies from their dressers and run to the shop to buy themselves sweeties, even though it was not Saturday. Children hurriedly did as they were told, knowing that they had already heard and seen too much. The women's lips were sealed tight, knowing that the pipe had already burst and their tears were too late.

The earth should have opened up and enfolded Bake-Face. Instead, she protruded like the stump of a dead tree. All these years with these four women, being nothing more than an attentive ear, an echo, so that they could find their own meaning. Bake-Face was stung. She had accused Jennifer of nothing. Why drag Mr. Johnson into it? Didn't Jennifer and the others know that her relationship with Mr. Johnson was like an egg-shell? Especially this crop season, now that she was beginning to feel her time drawing to a close. Five months out of the year were not sufficient; it was too short a time to spend with the one she loved, but there was no solution—at least, she saw none. This was the realization that Bake-Face had arrived at, and it was like food caught in her throat: it just rested there, not coming up or going down, choking her. It was only this morning that Bake-Face had decided to tell Mr. Johnson that he fit like gloves on her hand, and the reason she kept coming to him every year was because she loved him. She wanted to be with him, to try the dream for a year, but here stood Jennifer treating her life like dirt. She had only just found it, and the courage to say it to herself, but Jennifer stood accusing her of theft and neglect. The moon was not even full, nor did an owl hoot lately, an omen of doom.

Bake-Face looked around, only meeting the sides of women's faces, so her eyes turned to the leaves heavy like hampers loaded with food for the market. To look was a load, a burden. She should have kept her heart sealed, but the incision had already been made, so now she would have to wait for healing.

Bake-Face placed her hands on her head and hollered. Joyce came to comfort her, but she pushed away, spinning around and lamenting, doing what she never did twenty odd years ago when her mother and father died in the hurricane, their boat caught at sea. She wept for the rapes she had suffered silently from one uncle after another, for floggings she had endured from one aunt to another, for the jeers and abuse she had suffered from cousins and peers who ostracized her, forcing her into silence. Her shriek was for all these things and other things unsaid; it was for twenty-five years of suffering after she was left an orphan at ten.

The women formed a circle around Bake-Face, sucking in their own tears as Bake-Face spun around like a dog dying of fits. Finally, she collapsed on the ground, and the day turned grey.

Silence hung around Bruk-up House like the smell of mothballs in grandma's drawers. It was indeed pungent. The children and domestic animals smelled it. Not even breathing could be heard. The children refrained from sucking their snow-ball and ice-mints, not tasting the sweetness. Their eyes, however, were loud as they looked at their mothers. They knew that the slightest movement on their part would solicit a harsh spanking from any or all of the women. Even the dogs were cautious and kept their distance, crawling to the front of the yard to lie quietly by the flowerbeds.

Finally, Bake-Face hauled herself up, headed straight for her room, and shut herself in, not emerging for the remainder of the day. The chain was broken and the women mourned, not ending their grief even when their men returned from work and they went to their respective rooms. The men and children took the cue from the women and joined in the wake. Already the incident had spread like fire through Noman Estate.

The next morning, Thursday, Bake-Face tottered from her room, her head tied and the smell of bay rum loud about her person. The women stood by their kitchen doors and waited. Joyce nodded to Jennifer, who tried in the awkward fashion which was a part of her young nature to solder the link, but Bake-Face looked right through her and moved to her own kitchen without acknowledging anyone, and the women watched and waited. Finally, they shook their heads, knowing that time is iodine on a blistering sore.

With Bake-Face's refusal to make amends, Jennifer lost all hope, especially in view of the fact that last night Peter did not come home: he was not on the graveyard shift and her gungu rice and peas had burned. Distraught, she went to sit by her kitchen door, her head low in her lap. She did not understand Maud's power over Peter. All of the women of Bruk-up House agreed that she was the most attractive—pleasingly plump—not fat like Bridget or mawga like Bake-Face. Besides, she always spent the time to make herself appealing, even following Joyce's suggestion to dab perfume behind her ears and other places in the manner of the women in the magazines. Yet, in spite of all her efforts, Maud with her mountainous rear and jack-fruit breasts had her man.

Failing to make peace at home, Jennifer decided to go and have a talk with her rival. As she approached the barracks, she saw Peter leaving Maud's building. Salt blinded her eyes. She stopped to hide behind one of the buildings so that Peter wouldn't see her. In front of Maud's building was a tamarind tree. Jennifer broke off a piece of switch as she charged toward Maud's room, who greeted her at the door wearing only a thin nightie, revealing her to be an elephant. "Is yuh man yuh lookin fah, me love?" Maud mocked, her laughter vibrating like a ripe bread-fruit falling to the ground. Jennifer boiled. What did Peter see in Maud? Her skin was ash-colored and coarse, her face round like bulla-cake, her teeth jagged. What was it that appealed to men? Jennifer could not see it. Maud was easy and willing, and that was all the encouragement men needed. Jennifer's only concern was Peter; she kept herself for him, even though many men had made passes at her, and until this affair with Maud, she was certain Peter had kept himself for her—such was her reasoning. When she spoke to Maud, her words were more of a plea: "Ah wan yuh fi leabe me man alone." Maud roared: "Gal, if yuh nuh ave wha fi keep man, nuh come beggin fah sympathy." Jennifer raised the tamarind switch and Maud shouted. Jennifer brought it down, and Maud ran as fast as her legs could move around the barracks. Jennifer was after her; Maud bawled and hollered for help. Women, men and children stopped to watch, but no one came to Maud's aid. Jennifer hit her on her legs and she fell to the ground. Then, the flogging began.

Jennifer got on Maud's back, raised her nightie and whipped her like a child, all the while warning her: "Ah seh yuh fi stop shakin yuh ass in de face of ooman men." Maud, a notorious coward, hollered and rolled in the dirt. The women of the barracks cheered, and Jennifer got more excited. The children giggled and pointed and the men hung their heads, their big toes pressing into the soil.

The tamarind switch sliced into Maud's skin, bringing blood. She hollered louder, calling on her children and their nameless fathers for protection: "Dats enuf, daughta, dats enuf."

The women pulled Jennifer from Maud. One wiped her face with her apron and the others put their hands on her for support. Jennifer at once felt diminished for fighting like a common fishwoman and exalted for fighting for what was hers. Using the back of her hand, she wiped her tears, raised her head and spoke to the women who gathered. "Peta is good man. Im tek care a me an we picknie dem. Im neba stray til now. Ebery marnin me wake up is fi im one face me smile pan. Im is de only man who breathe hot air pan me neck-back a nite, an is so me wan eh fi continue." Then, turning to where Maud still lay, she warned, "Yuh is wukless whore; yuh did inveigle me man an me nah guh put up wid eh. If yuh trow yuh ass in any ooman man face again, we a guh peppa yuh like dem use to duh whore."

With this, Jennifer left the barracks to the applause of the inhabitants, who all turned away from Maud, but took her children along with theirs to feed. The news preceded Jennifer to Bruk-up House; when she appeared, the women acknowledged her with bold smiles, nodding their heads approvingly, but hers hung low as she mounted the stairs to her apartment. Seeing Peter with Maud's sweat still on his body dozing on her bed made Jennifer's blood boil all over. The tamarind switch itched in her hand. She raised it above her head and it came down with a tiger's force on Peter's back. He hollered and jumped up. Jennifer ignored him, raising the switch again. It landed across his stomach. Drunk with stupor and fatigue, he stumbled. Each time, Jennifer connected at a new and tender spot. Jennifer no longer saw Peter; all she saw was his namesake, their eight-year-old son whom she had beaten in a very cruel fashion a year ago, when he went off all day until late at night without telling her, returning with a carefree jig. All day she had seen his body devoured by alligators at the swamp, run over by a motorcar on the main road, washed away at sea by currents or broken into pieces falling from a cliff. Yet here he was eleven-thirty at night with no explanations, wearing triumph on his face while she had experienced many deaths all that day. She was relieved to see him, but she wanted him to comprehend her anxieties, so she flogged him until Bake-Face came and pulled the child away, keeping the boy in her room with her and Mr. Johnson that night. It was a similar sensation that went through Jennifer's body as the switch came down on Peter and all his barking threats that she was crazy, that he was going to bust her lips and knock out her teeth when he was rested, went in one ear and out the other.

Everyone in Bruk-up House left off their chores and games and sleep to listen, but no one laughed, at least not openly, because Jennifer and Peter were part of their family—their friends, people they loved and respected. The men listened closely, wondering about the wrath of their own women, and their women, who had only seen their strength as their capacity to withstand, now embraced Jennifer's act as their victory. The children were puzzled, but taking the cue from their mothers, they were zealous in their play.

Jennifer ordered Peter to go downstairs and wash the whore's filth from his body. She followed him, then sat under the mango tree and had a good cry.

Bake-Face, startled by such a demonstration of woman's will, crept to her room, doubting that she could be that forceful, even to keep Mr. Johnson. The other women did not openly cheer Jennifer, but one brought her a glass of limeade, another brought her food, a third brought her a towel, and Joyce rubbed her hand with bay rum. The men walked to safer backyards to play dominoes, and the children ran to the commons to play.

Peter crawled from the shower, his body waled and swollen. He went to where Jennifer sat, put his arms about her, and together they cried. Then, supporting each other, they entered their apartment, closing the door behind them. For the remainder of the day, they were not seen nor was a squeak heard from them, not even at two o'clock when it was time for Peter to go to work, so Richard was summoned to do his shift.

The next morning, Jennifer was up early singing a gallant calypso. Joyce, whose apartment was below Peter and Jennifer's, told the women that for the greater part of the night Jennifer's bed creaked, causing her to get very little sleep. Unable to restrain herself, Jennifer joined the women in laughter and they embraced her, all except Bake-Face, who was still nursing her wounds.

All of this Bake-Face now re-experiences as she sits under the mango tree waiting for Mr. Johnson to come home. She looks up at the sky and sees the stars. It is too late to make a wish. What to wish for, anyway? Can she be different with Mr. Johnson? Could they set up a permanent house and be content with each other the year round? She fears the uncertainty and so withdraws: "Love is like a gerba plant, yes; eh bloom, den die, den bloom again." She is no Jennifer; she doesn't know how to fight. Bake-Face smiles a sad smile: "Jen-

nifa alrite, yes, she will get all er wants an more."
Again, she nods her head and clears her throat: "Some
ooman born fi win an odas . . . " She does not complete
her thought as Jennifer, on her way to the bathroom,
stops in front of her.

For an awkward moment, the women stare at
each other, neither blinking, but Bake-Face is the first
to lower her eyes. Jennifer swings her arms; then, she
attempts to make contact: "Howdy, Bake-Face." Bake-
Face nods her head—the words are caught in her belly.
Jennifer takes the gesture as encouragement. Again
she clears her throat. "Bake-Face," she begins, looking
the woman squarely in the eyes. "Ah been knowin yuh
dese five years an de truth is ah don undastan yuh
nun. Ah did wrong a while back talkin to yuh de way
ah did, but de truth is ah nuh regret it." Joyce, standing
in the shadow, strains her ears. Jennifer continues.
"Yuh see, Bake-Face, ah did like yuh fah true. One
ting wid all we ooman ere—we like each oda, dats why
we nuh ave nuh contention inna de yard. But anyway—
yuh, well, funny. Is like yuh nuh feel yuh deserve nutten. Waheva yuh wan do wid Missa Johnson is fih yuh
business, but ah tink yuh know widin yuh heart of
heart dat time come fi yuh fi act." This is met only by
silence and eyes that are the pit of a river-bed. So deep
is Bake-Face's suffering that Jennifer tastes it on her
tongue and her stomach grumbles in protest. Still,
Bake-Face says nothing. "Bake-Face," Jennifer jars her
from the road she has wandered on, "Ah wan yuh fi
know how ah feel, an ah nuh wan we fi part wid nuh
bad feelins cause we guh back too far, and we neba
vex each oda fore, and me will neba faget how yuh did
save me from beatin me own picknie tuh death, suh
me aguh talk to yuh even if yuh nuh ansa me back."

Bake-Face shifts her weight. Joyce's neck is a
giraffe's. Jennifer stands with her hands akimbo. She
is for true a guava woman—smooth outside and
sweeter inside; the men's glances have all confirmed
this. Bake-Face chews her gum. A tractor rolls by. Looking off into the distance, Bake-Face clears her throat:
"Jennifa, me nuh vex yuh long time now. Yuh is peppa;

yuh is yuh own ooman. Long time now, me nuh me own ooman. Time well late. Nuh peppa nuh inna me; me kyan hole on to meself, but yuh fi keep clutchin. Yuh is ooman, yuh is yuh own ooman fi true." They squeeze hands. Joyce sighs with relief and turns back to her room, forgetting where she was heading.

Bake-Face walks to the middle of the yard, where the dirt is smooth and the children always play marbles and hop-scotch. She stoops, doodling in the dirt with her fingers. Peter, returning from work, greets Bake-Face. She responds with a nod and her mournful smile. He ascends the stairs. Bake-Face chuckles. Ever since that Thursday morning, he has been coming home straight after work, and he and Jennifer are closer. Only yesterday Bake-Face heard whispers of marriage. It isn't that the official paper is important, but often it is a public acknowledgement of bonding. Anyway, Jennifer and Peter are due, both in their late twenties with three children; the ritual would give their love a foundation. Again, Bake-Face chuckles. Maud is now sleeping with Bertram, the old, one-eyed garbage man who rumor claims is secretly rich.

Night has claimed the day. Men with their machetes swinging loosely have long gone home with the day's perspiration clinging to their clothes. The eight o'clock whistle sounds. Bake-Face looks in the direction of the factory. At this very moment, she imagines Mr. Johnson inspecting the boilers to make sure that the pot-boilers aren't taking too much sugar, molasses or cane-juice for their wives and sweethearts. Focusing on Mr. Johnson pains Bake-Face. Her eyes blur; she closes them tight like a constipated child sitting on the pot.

Crickets chatter, frogs and lizards croak, penewales dart—all the night creatures an orchestra. Bake-Face moves back to the mango tree and becomes a part of it. The question is still: should she return to Ezra and tell Mr. Johnson enough, or should she . . . what? She has never had choices up until now, and in fact, she isn't sure she is faced with a decision. What is it she is hoping for now, at this time in her life? This last year, Johnson has been telling her that when she smiles he sees a sunflower. Perhaps she thinks herself pretty. Perhaps she is throwing off her bruises; even Joyce commented that this year she is more talkative than usual. But that's what got her into trouble. Last year she would not have ventured to speak to anyone before being addressed, but only a month ago she initiated a conversation which threw all the inhabitants of Bruk-up House into confusion. That's over now; she and Jennifer are friends again, yet she doesn't trust herself. She needs more time to think, but the seven months away from Mr. Johnson are just too lonely. Ezra's goodness is a curse; she wishes he would abuse her so she could run away. How could she just pack up her things and walk? He took her in when she was at her lowest. Such ingratitude would surely fall down on her head, but to pack up again and go back? Pauline doesn't need her. There is a hurricane in her head.

She had been the only child; her parents were much older than other people with children in the village. So she was often teased that she had granny for parents. She remembered that school was closed because the headmistress said the radio warned of a storm. She and the other children hurried the six miles home through the bush on the gravel road. When she got home, she found the small two-room cottage in darkness, and was afraid. Her mother often accompanied her father, who was a fisherman, out to sea. She remembered the last night they left, telling her that they would be back that night or early the next morning. She was only ten, but long used to being by herself, as often her mother went with her father after making sure she had food to eat in their absence.

The winds started, then the thunder and lightning, and the rains began. She hid under the bed and fell asleep, waking only to find herself in water and half of the roof asunder. That was all she remembered and then the funeral, seeing her mother and father lying battered and bruised in their coffins, watching as they were lowered into the same hole and the men piled dirt on top of them. Hearing the people around her weeping, and not feeling anything. It wasn't her life anyway—she was never given life, just a shell, so she turned further inside herself, her eyes a muddy river, her body rigid, curled over like rubbish.

Joyce, on her way to the showers, flutters; a scream is somewhere in her body. She steadies herself, making out Bake-Face. "Lawd, God, Bake-Face, just now me did tink yuh was duppy. Lawd, me heart jus run to me mout bram."

In spite of herself, Bake-Face laughs at the thought of being mistaken for a ghost. It is Joyce she misses when she is away from Bruk-up House, sometimes more than Mr. Johnson. Joyce has a way of looking at things and making them right, without passing judgements as to right and wrong. As Joyce puts it, "Eberyting ave dem rite side an wrong side." Again, Bake-Face laughs. She motions to Joyce, who joins her, sitting squarely on her ample rear, raising her knees toward her chest and lapping her skirt between her legs as Bake-Face does, and as all women do who, when they sit, allow the breeze to cool their crotches.

Bake-Face takes Joyce's hands, which are warm and coarse. They become girls, whispering, making plans for the dolls they never had—their children—who are often more a burden than a blessing, and as for themselves, never time enough to sort out their feelings, never choices enough to choose, never idle moments to simply be. Bake-Face has always wanted a friend of her very own, someone special to share things with, but all during her short school days and when living with relatives as a young woman, that special friend never came. Then, when she was beginning to lose hope at thirty, her daughter was born. That was her first friend, but the friendship never had time to grow. Then she met Joyce. "Joyce, yuh know wha," Bake-Face speaks as if dreaming, "Pauline is de start of me entia life. Nutten neba appen to me good fore she born. Well, Ezra did okay. Den afta she come, eberyting appen at once. Me meet Johnson an you. Fi five mont out a de year me heart breade an get air. Why only now, Joyce? Why?" Joyce smooths Bake-Face's hair.

The night is their lover, so they respond to its beckoning. Joyce's voice is as soft as towels soaked in rainwater. "Bake-Face, is nuh crime fi love a man an wan fe be wid im. Look how long yuh an Johnson a galang." Bake-Face raises her hand in protest, but Joyce places it back in her lap. "Bake-Face, a time yuh an Johnson decide. People talk, but dem will always do dat, but yuh heart talk loudest. Listen to eh. Mek eh lead yuh like how water tek we spit an carry eh way." Bake-Face sucks on her pipe, even though all the tobacco is gone. She knocks it out on the trunk, then places it on a leaf beside her. Joyce's hand has grown sweaty. An owl hoots, startling Joyce, who pulls her hand free.

They listen to the night sounds. Many images flit through their minds. Then Bake-Face dozes. . . . She is riding a bicycle down a narrow strip of road that has no ending and she knows it. The more she rides, the narrower the road becomes; then suddenly, she is engulfed by canefields. Her bicycle disappears from under her. She keeps pedaling until she becomes a canestalk rooted to . . . She calls and calls to Mr. Johnson, but he does not hear her. The fields are burning. She smells the smoke as the fire closes in. . . .

Bake-Face clutches her throat and struggles; Joyce, hearing the shuffle of Mr. Johnson's steps, nudges Bake-Face, whose eyes are as frantic as a mad dog's. "Johnson ome," Joyce whispers, rising to take her shower. Bake-Face remains. Her left hand is behind her head, her right hand rests on her knees.

"Bake-Face!" It is Johnson calling; he sounds cross. She makes no reply. Johnson moves noisily about their apartment; she waits, holding her breath, knowing he will come to her and that she will not turn away from him. Shortly, Johnson's shadow emerges; she suppresses a giggle, which is new to her. Johnson looks around; his eyes adjust, seeing her.

Five years with Bake-Face have made Johnson very sensitive to her needs: he is not a communicative man; words are like bricks to him, but his senses are sharp, especially with Bake-Face. Approaching her, he lowers himself, making sure that his shoulder brushes against hers. Clearing his throat, he takes her hand, which immediately clasps his without a twitch, but her eyes are still turned to the sky as if seeking answers which do not exist.

He examines her profile by the moon. Puzzled, he wonders: "Why she keep comin back? Why she did come in de fus place?" He doesn't expect answers to these questions, but wonders whether he should ask her again to leave her husband and live with him. Rebecca would be content as long as he left her the farm, and though it is his life's savings, at forty, peace is more important. Should he suggest it again? The first time is still very vivid. Bake-Face was as cold as she was wild, almost petrified. He couldn't understand her reaction. All that day, she had stalked the room and not a word left her mouth for two whole days. Perhaps he should not broach the subject again; maybe next year, but he wants her so. She isn't rough and nagging like his wife; she accepts love gently, accepting guidance, yet demanding and directing it for her own pleasure. He knows there has been pleasure between them. They've had their moments. At times, he noticed her looking at him intently, like a dog staring at its own reflection in water, but if their eyes met at such times, Bake-Face would shrug her shoulder and look away; it was because she was afraid. He knows and understands, but he doesn't know how to help her claim herself and take what he is offering her.

Frank Johnson runs his hand through his hair. He notices Bake-Face nodding. "She is chile, yes," he mumbles. Bake-Face turns, resting her head on his shoulder. The fatigue of the long work shift walks through his body. He extends his legs in front of him;

he isn't one to delve into the past, or ponder for too long the inevitability of life. Johnson settles his head against the trunk and closes his eyes.

The myriad night sounds, the breeze and the fragrance of wet sugar and newly mown grass are agreeable. The moon wanders further on its course. The two sleep under the mango tree while duppies take possession of their empty bed.

Toward morning, chickens become restless, a rooster spreads its wings, puppies greedily suck their mothers' tits, a baby wakes for its 5:00 A.M. feed. The lizards have left off their croaking, men reach out for their women, and duppies are hastening to their graves as Bruk-up House unwinds. Snorers turn on their last round of sleep.

Bake-Face turns, hitting her head against the tree. She rubs her forehead. Already she feels a coco rising; the bump swells and is painful. A grey filter hangs before her eyes; she rubs them and her eyes roam the yard, bringing meaning to her location. By her side, Mr. Johnson snores with his mouth open. Feeling her pipe by her hand, Bake-Face places it in Mr. Johnson's open mouth, but he remains sleeping; she pushes it further, forcing a response. He chokes and coughs, and she smiles. He looks around: "Weh we de? Wha de time?" Bake-Face, her voice playful, teases: "Me look like time tuh yuh?" Johnson's voice, firm, rejoins: "Nuh boda wid de lip tonite. Come, mek we guh we bed." Rising, she adds: "Look like marnin to me. Duppy mus sleep inna we bed." She helps him to his feet. Taking a cue from her, he adds: "Den we will ave fi chase dem out wid some spirted rompin." She leads the way to their apartment.

Once inside, Johnson locks the door, but there is no need to turn any light on as the day's brightness is already penetrating. With her back to Johnson, Bake-Face slips out of her light cotton frock. She feels his eyes upon her and is suddenly shy, cupping her breast before slipping under the cover. Johnson watches all of this, seeing this side of her for the very first time. He takes long with his pants, then suddenly drops them, the belt buckle ringing throughout the room. Bake-Face turns her face to the wall. She reminds herself not to shrink from Johnson, and she knows that she won't because already her craving is hot. He slips out of his underpants. Bake-Face closes her eyes tight as he slides in beside her; she remains where she is, not allowing him much room; she feels his heat on her back and a shiver runs up and down her spine. Slowly his large hands move and cup her tiny breast, tenderly; then one hand travels to her waist; she trembles but tries to remain unaffected. He turns her towards him and kisses her forehead, then her breasts, allowing one hand to wander further. Bake-Face moans. She takes his hand and directs it. He resists momentarily, but she pulls his hand and guides it, reaching up her lips to taste his mouth. Tonight she will give herself as fully as she dares.

They meander; it becomes frantic, rolling around on the bed until they fall to the floor. She moans and her eyes swell with tears. She will take what she wants, she will walk outside of herself and taste the dawn. Johnson feels the tears in her eyes and pauses, but she pulls at him, responding yearningly to his fondling. He tries putting her on the bed, but she protests, guiding his hands once more, pulling him on top of her at the same time. She arches her buttocks from the floor, her tears flowing rapidly, but the sounds are all joyful as they clutch each other in a tight embrace.

Bake-Face turns in bed. The last thing she remembers was being on the floor and Johnson riding her. She turns and faces him. He is sound asleep and his forty years show. She gently caresses his face with her finger. He smiles and turns on his other side. She sighs. Last night or this morning completed everything. She took what she wanted. Lazily, she yawns and crawls out of bed.

At the showers, Bake-Face is greeted by Jennifer, who is singing another sassy calypso at the top of her voice. Bake-Face smiles at Jennifer, feeling somewhat akin to her. They hold each other around the waist and dance a few steps; Joyce watches them, then joins in the fun. Before long, the five women are singing at the top of their voices and doing a jig. Some man hollers: "Damn blast ooman, dem nuh gi yuh rest a nite an marnin dem start dem noise, like is dem one know good time." The women fan their hands in the direction of the voice and continue their song. Then they return to fixing breakfast. Bake-Face declares, "Jennifa, gal, ah gwane mek yuh some ah de bestest blue-drawers fore ah leabe."

The women rejoice, singing as they work. Bake-Face is long in the shower. Everything is right; she can leave now.

While she is wrapping the dough in the banana leaf which gives the blue-drawers their blue stain, Johnson joins her in the kitchen. He creeps up from behind her, hugs her by the waist and kisses her on her neck. Bake-Face jumps back and looks around to see if anyone saw them; he smiles at this and kisses her again. "Yuh fi get in de spirit more often," Johnson says with a big smile on his face, but to his surprise, Bake-Face snaps at him.

"Hush yuh mout; too late fah yuh to complain." He gestures with his hand, but decides to let it pass. The sweet smell of the blue-drawers enters his nostrils; he rubs his stomach. "How come yuh a mek dem today?" Johnson inquires, thinking the change of subject safe.

Her voice is still short. "Wha shift yuh pan?"

His shoulders question it, but he answers: "Two-to-ten." "Good, yuh won see me when me leabe," Bake-Face spits out, and it is like piss thrown in Johnson's face. His mouth twitches and his face becomes a mangled net in the sand. Bake-Face avoids his face. "Me a guh catch de aftanoon train," she manages matter-of-factly. Johnson scratches his head. Turning to face him, Bake-Face announces: "Me nuh come back nex year, suh yuh can begin fi fin anoda ooman fi care fah yuh." It was not what she wanted to say, but things are very confused.

Johnson stumbles from the kitchen and stands by the door. Why did he want her? The truth of the matter is that she didn't argue, but now he isn't sure; she didn't argue with noise, but rather with silence for which he could offer no reply or walk away from her in vexation. And now after truly giving herself to him, her noise is a rebuke: she has left no room for discussion; he is just a speck of dirt under her feet.

To whom hasn't he been a speck of dirt? With Bake-Face he had known something special; he couldn't say what, but that it was more than he had ever had he is certain. But here she is, forcing him back to his grave. His blood boils and with fist balled, he turns back to the kitchen. Her eyes like a stream greet him; she has moved back inside herself and nothing outside touches her. Johnson opens his fist and touches her face; tears are in his eyes; he isn't going to let it end like this. Stuttering, he pleads: "Bake-Face, why, why mus always be de same? Why? We is somebody, de sun shine pan we, too—why?" He waits for some gesture from her, but only her stare chastises him. Groping for control, his fists once again balled by his side, he mutters: "Man ave feeling tuh, yuh know; ooman neba did get de whole ah it fah demself." Still she says nothing and not a muscle moves in her face, and he senses her body rigid. "Bake-Face, talk to me, good God, talk to me; nuh let me eat yuh silence now." She shifts the weight of her body, but her lips are dry. Johnson is in her face; her hands are folded across her chest, refusing to let him in. He feels his palms sweaty, and perspiration mingles with his tears: "Me ave rass feelins fah yuh, Bake-Face, me ave feelins fah yuh." Their eyes stare into each other's; his are blinded with tears. Bake-Face runs her tongue over her lips and then replies: "Dat *good* dat yuh ave feelin, Johnson, dat *good*." Before he can control himself his fist slams her squarely in the chest, sending her reeling into the cupboard. The force is for twenty years of frustration. Bake-Face steadies herself, but she does not clutch at her chest, nor does she say anything. Johnson's fist aches and his head is a soccer ball being kicked around. He stares at Bake-Face, trying to find words, but her eyes, the vacant depth of a well, frighten him, so he flees from her kitchen.

Bake-Face stands by the window. A pigeon flaps on the sill and shits. The puppy has wandered in again and rubs its body against her foot. She picks it up: "Pauline gwane like yuh bad, gwane like yuh bad fi true." Then she puts it down and shoos it on its way. She finishes wrapping the blue-drawers and puts them on to bake. Tearing a piece of newspaper, she wipes away the pigeon shit. Two large black flies circle the kitchen. She knocks them to the floor, using the dish-pan cloth, and then she looks around. "Well, nuh need to pack—me won need dese ere tings nuhmore." Through the window, she notices the red peel-neck rooster pursuing the chicken; that is its life.

The sun bursts in, sets the kitchen afire. Bake-Face stands. Already she is at that narrow road; cane is all around her, allowing her no escape, and there is no Mr. Johnson to call out to.

· *Duppy Get Her* ·

Duppy nuh wan yuh drop
  yuh picknie deh, guh home
Duppy nuh wan yuh drop
  yuh picknie deh, guh home
Duppy nuh wan yuh drop
  yuh picknie deh, guh home, gal
tie yuh belly, gal, guh home.

*E*VENING falls like dewdrops on oleander petals glistening under the sun. Oshun, goddess of love, is present, her orange-yellow skirt swaying coquettishly. Mosquitoes are like kiskode petals on skin, blown off by the lax odor whispering mischief in the air. Cane fields rustle in frolic; answered by the evening breeze, they dance the merenge, twirling to giddiness. What are the cane fields saying? What is uttered by the leaves? Listen! Listen—with wide eyes.

Suddenly the murmur of the cane fields—almost hypnotic—forces everyone to look in their direction. Swirling, they sing:

Steal away, steal away;
  duppy gwana get yuh, gal, steal away.
Steal away, steal away;
  duppy a come get yuh, gal, steal away.

The labyrishers—gossipers—do not hear; they don't hear, save one—Lilly.

Lilly cleans house, cooks food, washes clothes, irons and does other domestic chores for her living. She has been since she was sixteen; she is eighteen, now, and with child due any day. She sits with Beatrice, her cousin, also a domestic; with Richard, her baby's father and a pot-boiler at the sugar estate; and with

Basil and Errol, two other factory hands. They are gathered together, feeling contented at being their own bosses for at least the next twelve hours.

The evening is rare in its simple grace. The sun, sinking beyond the cane fields, dominates the sky. All the land kneels in homage to this god of energy and sustainer of life—fully orange, gigantic and mystic, surrounded by black-purple haze. The clouds stand back, way off in respect. The sun, heedful of his power, gyrates and snarls. Lilly glances at him just as he flaps his ears, emitting fire from his nostrils; she checks her laughter. So awed is she by the sun's fire she scarcely breathes. After some moments, Lilly mumbles: "Lawd, de sun mitey tonite, sah. Look, im on im way home nuh." Suddenly, the turning of the child in her belly elicits a laugh that escapes deep from her womb.

Beatrice, seated by her, places her hand on Lilly's stomach, feeling the baby's position. "Dis a definite boy picknie yuh a guh ave. See how yuh belly pointed and de sonofabitch won gi yuh nuh peace."

"Im mus tek afta im fada."

Richard turns away in vexation; he chups, kissing his teeth: "Is me yuh ave mout fah, nuh? Ooman neba satisfy. Wen dem nuh ave nutten else fi seh, dem chat stupidness." He moves to leave, but changes his mind; he chups again: "Nuh boda me backside dis evenin yah, gal, nuh boda me backside."

The breeze whistles by. The dogs cover their ears in embarrassment, while the frogs exchange glances which ask, "What's troubling him this nice evening, eh? What's troubling him?" A green lizard, in response, croaks; its bulging eyes are lit by the sun. There is silence amidst the gathering of two women and three men—maids, pot-boiler and factory-hands.

Silence dominates but the undercurrent there is anger mingled with amusement and foreboding. Again, the swishing of the cane fields seems to grab everyone's attention. Lilly is rocking. Suddenly noticing a flock of birds in the sky, she points like an excited child. Again, silence. The sun is almost gone. Lilly sees a star, and thinking it must be the very first one in the sky this evening, she quickly makes a wish, anxious for its fulfillment. She resumes her rocking, forgetting what it was she wished for. A rooster cackles near the barbed wire fence separating them from the canal and the cane field beyond. Two dogs are stuck, one in the other.

Richard picks up a stone, throws it at them; he swears under his breath: "Damn dog—dem nuh ave nuh shame. Look how much bush bout de place, yet dem a fi come rite inna de open."

Beatrice snickers. Lilly retorts, "Nuh eberybode wait till nite fi cova dem act inna de darkness like yuh."

"Ooman, me nuh tell yuh nuh boda me soul-case. If yuh nuh ave nutten fi seh, shet yuh backside."

Beatrice comments, "Some people hot tonite, Lawd. Mus all dat boilin molasses. De sweetness keep de heat inna de body." Again silence. Beatrice fidgets in the chair, which is too small for her large behind. Suddenly, she starts singing, a mischievous smile on her face. Her voice is full and melodious, and her song is aimed at Richard, whom she always provokes to anger:

> Gentle Jesas, meek an mile,
>   look upon a trouble man.
> Ease im soul an let im rest,
>   for im is a soul distress.

Lilly bursts out in loud belly-laughter and Errol and Basil sputter. Richard's color is rising like the pink of a cat's tongue. Anger is clearly written on his face. A sudden wind blows dirt into Beatrice's eye, putting an end to her song.

Richard keenly observes the little gathering and feels excluded. He looks at the dark bodies, envying them. He is the "red nega" among them. All during his school days, the boys teased him, saying his mother had slept with a sailor. And even though he knew it wasn't true (although he was the fairest one in his family), he was still always hurt; he didn't care if his great-great-grandfather had married an Irish settler whom he resembled. He wanted to be purple-dark like the rest of them so his face wouldn't turn red like the color of sorrel fruit whenever he got angry. Staying out in the sun didn't help either; it only made his skin tomato. Lean and muscular, he stood out like a guinep among star-apples.

Lately, however (that is, ever since meeting Lilly not yet twelve months ago), Richard has been relaxed. Lilly, lusted after by all the men, the gentlemen of the community included, chose him. Although every once in a while she teases him about his complexion and stings his hand to see her fingerprints revealed, he knows she cares for him.

Richard doesn't feel like being anyone's beating stick tonight, however. He looks from Lilly, sitting with a smile crowning her face, to Errol and Basil, with mischief twinkling in their eyes, to Beatrice, playing her usual pious role. Richard wants to remind Beatrice of the nightly utterances of her mattress and bedsprings, but he holds his tongue as he isn't sure whether it is Errol or Basil or both who pray to the Lord between her thighs at night. He chuckles, stomping the balls of his feet, and then chups, kissing his teeth, before turning to fidget with his bicycle. "One of des days oonuh gwane wan fi serious and kyan," he warns.

Richard catches a glimpse of the sun just before it disappears, and it whispers to him: "Steal away, steal away—duppy gwane box yuh, duppy nuh like yuh, steal away . . . " He looks over his shoulder to see if anyone else heard. No one did; the group is already onto something else.

The cane fields whimper, swishing to and fro. The evening is alive. All the creatures stop to say their piece. Sparkling fireflies called penewales dart in and out of the darkness; crickets are in argument. Even the water in the canal tastes the omen. It rumbles like a vexed child who is sent to sweep up the dirt and gather leaves; the task adds to the child's vexation when the twirling leaves blind his eyes while playing rounders with the breeze. So is the evening sweet yet wicked—as

46

even the nicest woman can be.

The rustling of the cane fields is louder. Beatrice shivers. Blossoms from the ackee tree fall and the wind takes them, blowing them everywhere. Lilly tries to catch the blossoms, but the movement in her belly stops her. She relaxes and pats her stomach.

Beatrice feels her head growing big; it is a ton of bricks on her body. She rubs her arms, feeling the cold-bumps. Something is going to happen. She looks around at Richard, who is still angry, and Basil and Errol, who are sharing some private joke. Beatrice reaches over and rubs Lilly's belly, feeling the child inside kicking. She is certain it's a boy. Again, the murmur of the cane fields. Beatrice quickly blows into her cupped palms and throws the air over her left shoulder. It is her way of telling the duppies to step back. She cannot see the ghosts, but she senses their presence near. Again she cups her palms, blows, and throws her cupped hands over her right shoulder, cursing a bad-word with the motion before mumbling "De Lawd is me Shepherd, Ah fear nuh evil. . . . " Still she senses an outside force. Lilly is smiling to herself and rocking, one hand patting her stomach.

Beatrice's head swells; she feels it's much larger than her body, much larger than the veranda where they are sitting, much larger than the evening. She hugs her bosom and rocks, trying to put aside the fear that has crept upon her without invitation.

After her mother died when she was six and her father wandered to another town and another woman, Beatrice was taken in by Lilly's mother, who was her aunt. She was two years older than Lilly, so their lives followed similar paths until at fifteen Beatrice's was partially ruined by her Sunday school teacher. Fear made her keep her mouth shut; prayer made the child born dead. Soon thereafter she left, getting several jobs as domestic help before settling in this quiet community. Eight years ago, Beatrice and Lilly both attended their grandparents' funerals, three months apart. They were always close, so over the years, they kept in touch. When Lilly complained of being restless and wanting to leave the overprotective shield of her mother two years ago, Beatrice found her a job with her own employer Mrs. Edwards. That was how they came to be together again.

Before Beatrice lost her child, she had promised the Lord that she would spread his name if he killed the life that was growing in her womb. When the child was born strangled, she kept her word, but it was already too late, because she had discovered the joy which lay buried between her legs. As she wasn't pretty, it was easy to have several men without ruining her reputation. No one wanted to boast of sleeping with the coarse, big busted, no ass, Jesus-crazy maid. This way she had it her way all the time, not really trusting any man in the first place.

Putting aside her reflections, Beatrice leans her head to hear what Basil is saying.

"Oonuh look like oonuh inna anoda world."

Richard is still fidgeting with his bicycle; Errol has gone to help him. Lilly, rocking on the seatless cane rocker, is hypnotized by the rustling cane field beyond. Beatrice and Basil notice her staring at what to them appears to be nothing. They feel her strangeness like silence between them. Pausing to take it in, they resume their conversation. An ackee blossom falls, disquieting Richard, and he curses: "See yah, Lawd, yuh nuh test me fait tuh dis yah nite."

A man and woman have crept out of the cane field. They stand right at the edge on the bank of the canal. To look at the woman is to see an older Lilly. The man is all grey. The woman wears a plaid dress gathered at the waist, and her feet are without shoes. Her husband wears rubber shoes and stained khaki pants turned up at the ankles. His faded shirt is partially unbuttoned, his arm is around his wife's waist. They exude a gentleness like the petals of roses. The woman uses her index finger to beckon to Lilly. Jumping as if pulled from her seat, Lilly bounds toward the man and woman by the cane field beyond the canal and beyond the barbed wire fence. She scrambles over Beatrice's feet.

Beatrice yells, "Lilly, Lilly, weh yuh a guh? Lilly! Is mad? Yuh mad? Min yuh fall down hurt yuhself. Lilly! Gal, weh yuh a guh?"

Richard runs after Lilly.

Beatrice repeats, "Lilly, gal, wha get inna yuh?"

Lilly: "Yuh rass-cloth, leabe me alone. Yuh nuh ear me granny a call me?" She points to what appears to be the canal.

They all stare, seeing no one, hearing nothing. Lilly is close to the fence, running, tearing off her clothes. Fearing that she is going to dive in, Richard reaches for her, but she clutches and attempts the barbed wire fence; Richard pulls at her. She boxes and derides him till he releases her. She tries scrambling through. Richard takes firm hold of her and pulls her safely from the fence. Beatrice is by their side; she helps with Lilly. Errol stands transfixed by the bicycle, while Basil cranes his neck from the veranda. Richard and Beatrice struggle with Lilly, pulling her away from the fence; they are breathless, but luckily, Lilly settles down for a moment.

The woman in the cane field beckons to Lilly, cajoling: "Lilly, me picknie, come kiss yuh granny and granpa; yuh nuh long fi see we?"

Lilly, strident, gesticulates wildly like a man cheated out of his paycheck. She calls, "Yes, Granny, me a come, me long fi see yuh."

Beatrice and Richard struggle with Lilly. Their fright and confusion are as loud as Lilly's screams. Richard tries to rough her up but she merely bucks him off. Beatrice's jaws work, sweat forms on her forehead, and her fleshy arms flail about, comical.

Again, she tries to reason with Lilly: "Lilly, gal, memba me and you did help dress Granny fah er funeral? Memba, memba, Lilly, how we did cry til we eye swell big? Granny dead. She nuh call yuh."

"Granny nuh dead; see, she stan deh wid granpa. Oonuh leh me guh." At this, Lilly spits at Beatrice and Richard and frees herself from their hold.

She rushes toward the cane field like a man afire

in search of water. Richard seizes her, but she now has the strength of many persons; he hollers for Errol and Basil. Lilly rips off her blouse and brassiere, and her ample breasts flap about. Richard remembers the taste of her milk, only last night. More hands take hold of her; she bites, scratches and kicks. Miss Maud from next door, hearing the commotion, runs to her fence to learn all about it.

"Leh me guh, leh me guh! Yuh nuh see me granny a call me? Leh me guh."

Richard: "Lilly, shet yuh mout. Min Miss Edward ear yuh an yuh loose yuh wuk. Nuhbody nuh call yuh."

"Miss Edward bumbu-hole—Miss Edward rass-cloth. Oonuh leabe me alone mek me guh tuh me granny and granpa."

Beatrice scolds: "Lilly, gal, shet yuh mout. How yuh can speak suh bout Miss Edward? Gal, shet yuh mout for yuh loose yuh wuk."

"Oonuh rass-cloth, oonuh bumbu-hole, oonuh leabe me alone—mek me guh to me granny."

The four find it difficult to hold Lilly. She kicks, bucks and tears at her remaining clothes. The evening sings:

Steal away, steal away, duppy get yuh.
Steal away . . . duppy get yuh . . .

From across the fence, Miss Maud offers: "Lawd, God, duppy done mad me picknie, Lawd God. Jesas! Rub er up wid some frankincense and white rum; rub er up quick come." Before anyone can respond, she is climbing through the barbed wire fence which separates her yard from theirs, opening a bottle. In her haste, her dress catches on the fence, but she pulls it, ripping the hem. The pungent smell from the bottle vapors into the air.

Miss Maud rubs Lilly's hands, face and neck with the potion, then makes the sign of the cross in the air. Now she sprinkles some of the substance on the ground, muttering: "Steal away, duppy, steal away. De deed well done; steal away. . . . " She looks about her, pats her head and turns to Beatrice. "Fin piece a red rag, tie er head. Duppy fraid red, fraid red. Our Fada who in heaven, duppy fraid red. Dy kingdom come, tie er head. Dy will be done, tie er head. Ave mercy, Pupa Jesas."

Lilly breathes heavily; Richard, Errol and Basil hold her firmly.

Says Beatrice, "She kyan stay ere; dem nuh wan er stay ere."

Maud explains, "Dem jus wan er home. No arm will be done. Lawd ave mercy."

Richard stares at Lilly: "Who obeah me sweet Lilly? Who?"

Beatrice explodes: "Shet yuh mout, Richard, nuhbody nuh set nuh spell pan Lilly, nuhbody obeah er."

> *Steal away, chile, steal away.*
> *Duppy nuh wan yuh ere, chile,*
> *duppy nuh wan yuh ere.*
> *Dem nuh wan yuh ere.*

It is generally agreed that Lilly must be returned to her place of birth—that for whatever reason, her dead grandparents don't want her where she is. Mrs. Edwards is consulted and a car is summoned. Kicking and frothing at the mouth, Lilly is forced into the back of the car, Richard to her right and Basil to her left. Beatrice sits up front with the driver armed with Miss Maud's flask of potion. The car pulls off, leaving a trail of dust.

Mrs. Edwards returns to her house; she fumbles inside her medicine cabinet and comes up with a brown vial, the contents of which she sprinkles at each doorway and window and in all four corners of every room. Then she goes back to her rocking chair, her hands folded in her lap, her eyes searching the grey sky.

Miss Maud, the community myalist—healer—returns to her backyard. Her lips are pouted and her eyes intent, as if seeking a shiny shilling in the road; she shakes her head from side to side.

Suddenly she is possessed; she twirls around her

yard, her wide skirt billowing out, her hands lifted to the sky, her feet marching time to an invisible drum. Her voice, deep bass, echoes like a man's throughout the entire community:

> Duppy nuh wan yuh drop
>   yuh picknie deh, guh home
> Duppy nuh wan yuh drop
>   yuh picknie deh, guh home
> Duppy nuh wan yuh drop
>   yuh picknie deh, guh home, gal,
>   tie yuh belly, gal, guh home.
> Yuh muma seh she neba raise
>   nuh picknie fi guh lego
> Yuh muma seh she neba raise
>   nuh picknie fi guh lego
> Yuh muma seh she neba raise
>   nuh picknie fi guh lego
>   tie yuh belly, guh home.
> Duppy nuh wan yuh drop
>   yuh picknie deh
>   tie yuh belly, guh home.
> Guh home.

Mrs. Edwards feels cold-bumps covering her arms as she watches Miss Maud twirling and singing in her yard. The swishing of the cane fields has stopped and suddenly, a sense of desolation—abandonment—takes over. The sky turns a deep mauve, a lone donkey somewhere in the distance brays, brays, brays and the night is on so fully all creep to the safety of their homes and pull the covers tightly over their heads. Only Mrs. Edwards sits for a long time on her veranda in the dark, rocking and rocking away the fear and doubt.

Upon returning from taking Lilly home, Beatrice reports that Lilly calmed gradually as she approached her place of birth. In fact, by the time she got home, she was reasonable enough to request from her mother a cup of water sweetened with condensed milk . After drinking the milk, Lilly hugged her mother and they both cried; no one had to restrain her thereafter. Nothing needed to be explained to Lilly's mother, who had been expecting them all day. It appeared she had had a dream from her dead mother the night before.

Prior to this incident, Lilly always claimed that she saw duppies in Mrs. Edwards's house and around the estate in general. Since no one else professed such powers, there was no way to verify her claim. Many came to her when they wanted to ask for protection from those in the other world . Often, when they were in Lilly's presence, they asserted that they felt their heads rise and swell to twice their size, but again, since this was only a feeling and nothing visible, nothing could be proven. There were others who wanted to be able to see duppies like Lilly and asked her how they could obtain such powers. Lilly's recommendations were the following: "Rub dog matta inna yuh eye or visit a graveyard wen de clock strike twelve midnite. Once dere, put yuh head between yuh legs, spit, then get up an walk, not lookin back. Afta dat, yuh will see duppy all de time."

It is not known if anyone ever followed Lilly's advice, although two women who went to see Lilly had taken to visiting the graveyard daily and were now in the habit of talking to themselves.

Lilly returns to Mrs. Edwards's employment exactly ten weeks after the incident, healthy and as sane as before, with her bubbling, carefree manner. She gave birth to a seven-and-a-half pound boy, the spitting image of Richard, the day after her departure. The child was left behind with her mother, who christened him Sam, after his deceased grandfather.

Now when Lilly looks into the cane field, nothing bursts forth and no dead are brought back to life, but every time people see her looking, they remember that evening and somehow, the cane field starts rustling and a voice much like Lilly's rings throughout the entire community, stopping people at their chores:

Leh me guh, leh me guh, oonuh rass-cloth!
Le me guh—me granny a call me, oonuh leh me guh.
Mrs. Edwards bumbu-hole; leh me guh.

No one referred to Mrs. Edwards, a highly respected member of her community, in such a manner before, and no one has after Lilly. Lilly, of course, apologized to Mrs. Edwards, who graciously forgave her as she was not in possession of herself at the time. And although Mrs. Edwards was committed to taking Lilly back in her employment after she gave birth, whenever Mrs. Edwards was around her, she was always full of trepidation.

Lilly goes off one other time since the cane field incident. Several years have passed; Lilly is getting married to Richard. This is the big day. She is dressed, waiting to be taken to the church. Her grandmother appears again, but this time alone. Lilly rips her bridal dress to shreds and runs naked to the river, cursing everyone she meets, while Richard waits by the altar. For nine days she has to be tied down with ropes. For nine days, the breeze sings:

Steal away, steal away.
Duppy seh nuh, duppy seh nuh.
Steal away . . .

Lilly's face is a dimpled cake pan. Her body is pleasing like a mango tree laden with fruits. She has eight children, now, six for her husband and two for Richard, the first two. Richard stole away after duppy boxed him the second time. The last that was heard of him, it was reported that he was seen walking and talking to himself, his hair matty and his skin black from dirt. Lilly now has a maid to help her with her many chores; her husband owns a fleet of trucks.

Beatrice has opened up a storefront church in another community far from where the main part of this story took place. Her congregation is said to be ninety-two percent sturdy black men. Basil is still working as a pot-boiler at the sugar factory. Errol went abroad to England, it could be Canada or America as well, where he is said to have married an East Indian girl, so now he eats with his fingers.

After Lilly left Mrs. Edwards's employment, Mrs. Edwards swore confidentially to Mrs. Salmon, her best friend, that she would never again hire a maid from Agusta valley—that was the district from which Lilly came. Mrs. Edwards, of course, did not admit to a belief in local superstitions.

At least once a year, Miss Maud can still be heard singing at the top of her voice:

> Duppy nuh wan yuh drop
>   yuh picknie deh, guh home
> Duppy nuh wan yuh drop
>   yuh picknie deh, guh home
> Duppy nuh wan yuh drop
>   yuh picknie deh, guh home, gal,
>   tie yuh belly, guh home.

· Me Man Angel ·

"*I* REMEMBER Perry's eyes, his little face illuminated more than the moon. I sure love that little boy, love him to distraction." Mrs. Taylor grows silent and averts her eyes, afraid to look at Denise, not wanting to see her own tears mirrored in Denise's eyes.

Denise sighs, wipes her eyes and forces a smile. "De little time Perry spen wid me was special. Im gi me somtin nuhone or nuh time can tek way. Dat is love an fulfillment." The two women hold hands and pass the rest of the afternoon trying to outdo each other recounting their happy times with Perry. Every so often, they fall silent as each tries to imagine what Perry is doing now.

And so it is, wherever two or more women gather in the community of Monstrance, their talk always comes around to Perry—to the love they feel for him and to the great emptiness that his going leaves. The men, speaking with more bravado, reminisce about Perry as pause to their money worries or between gulps of rum or banging of dominoes on the table. The children, too, participate, making up stories about Perry and all his antics so that every detail about him spreads like the dazzling yellow-orange love-bush that overgrows hedges. Perry is already a folk hero and infants are put to bed with his tales. Much, much later in the future, the newer generation of Monstrance won't be quite sure if Perry really existed or whether he was merely a fabrication.

Monstrance is a rural community with no major agricultural crop to call attention to itself. Its residents, living some thirty miles from any town or urban center, spend their Saturdays and Sundays strolling along

Main Street, the only fully paved street in the community and the one that intersects two major roads that are partly paved. Top Lane is where the poorer inhabitants of this district live, and Bottom Valley is reserved for the more affluent. However, no one in Monstrance is rich; there are simply those who have a little bit more than the others.

Dennis and Denise MacFarlane live in the largest house on Bottom Side Lane with their nine children, over six dozen rabbits, two hundred chickens, four roosters, a flock of pigeons and a big backyard with many fruit trees and plenty of space for their children to play in. Their house is a sprawling, five-bedroom wooden structure with a large veranda both in front and in back.

Denise once confided to Miss Bridget, her next-door neighbor and best friend, that she resents all her children with the exception of Trevor and Linda—the two oldest. She feels that her other seven children forced themselves on her without giving her time to prepare for them. Trevor and Linda are dear to her because when they were conceived, she and Dennis were still lovers. Even after Linda was born, Dennis still clung to her passionately and every night after the table was cleared, they would nestle up and he would fall asleep on her bosom.

Then a third child came, soon a fourth, and the number kept increasing; Dennis shifted all his attention to his children and they became his passion. He swells with pride as he counts all his children and recalls their various peculiarities. Denise often watches him when he is glorying in his children with a look of disgust on her face. It is only nights when the children are snoring in their beds that Denise turns affectionately to her husband, but even in the privacy of their bed the children intrude, arousing resentment and jealousy in her.

"But Trevor an Linda special." Denise remembers how Trevor's love of breast feeding and Linda's habit of playing with her neck gave her deep satisfaction. She didn't have time to develop a relationship with the other children because all they seemed to want was to be fed and left alone to play among themselves. She wanted to experience deeply those lives which came pushing and screaming out of her, but somehow failed, so after nine children she still felt hollow, unfulfilled. While Dennis was a shepherd among his flock, she kept waiting for someone or something to come to her to fill the emptiness.

> *Nimble-timble hands*
> *Nimble-timble legs*
> *Soldier man needs sticks to play his drum*
> *Give him your nimble-timble hands and legs.*

Looking more like a precocious three-year-old than his six years, Perry is the wistful boy everyone knows and loves. Abandoned by his parents, who left him to be lost among his aunt and uncle's nine children, Perry looks like a discarded dishrag in comparison to the other healthy, active children. However, he is not neglected or abused; in fact, he is given more attention and care than any of the others.

Since birth, asthma and other serious ailments have plagued Perry so that he is always in an undershirt in the nearly 90-degree weather, even when everyone else is sweating and stripped to the bare essentials. His thin body looks undernourished and overworked, but his face has the delicate elegance of a petal floating in a barrel of rain water. His complexion has the strong assurance of lignumvitae wood; his woolly hair is cropped close to his skull, complementing his keenly etched features. All the muscles in Perry's forehead stand out like tracks. When women look into his forlorn face, his languid eyes, they take him into their arms and bury his head in the crevice of their breasts in an attempt to shield him from the world. Even the men abandon their unemotional exterior: stopping to take Perry in their arms, they rock him like an infant or hold him like a frail figure of straw.

For a long time, Perry does not attend school with Denise's other children. Instead, he stays home with his aunt and her two sets of twins. While the twins play in the dirt and make mud-puddings, Perry sits under a tree or on a stool in the kitchen, hanging onto his aunt's frock-tail. At lunch-time, Denise places the two sets of twins on the veranda to sit on an old sheet where they can make a mess with their meal and then takes Perry under the shade of a tree, where she holds him in her lap and spoon feeds him. Afterwards, she rocks him in her arms until he falls asleep.

Perry is the only one whose water is warmed for his bath. Not even the two sets of twins, who are eighteen months and three years respectively, get such treatment. All her children ceased to have their water warmed once they got to be one year old, but every morning after her five oldest children are off to school and every afternoon before they return, she puts on the large pot of water to boil for Perry's bath. Denise undresses Perry inside the house and wraps him in a towel before bringing him out on the back veranda to soak in his tub of warm water. His entire cleansing is a ritual. She always lights a white candle and puts blue in Perry's water to keep away evil spirits. Then, ever so gently, she cups her hands and pours water on his shoulders and back. After a few moments of this intimate exchange, she lathers her hands with soap and gingerly rubs the outlines of his body, acting as if his skin might fall off and dissolve in the water.

After the bath, Denise wraps Perry in a towel, takes him into her room and lays him on her bed as if she were setting down an egg. (Perry sleeps in the same room as his aunt and uncle, on a cot away from the window, because Denise fears the night draft might make him worse.) Then, wielding her towel like a blotter, she pats him dry. She oils his entire body, taking the time to massage his joints, rub his chest with tiger-balm, and brush his hair until the woolly naps move like the waves of the ocean. Twice daily, Perry goes through this quasi-religious exercise with a calm and oblivious attitude.

After more than a year of Denise's devotion, Perry has become more active, although he hasn't gained any weight, but now he plays with the twins, who are preparing for nursery school. At last, Perry has learned to skip and to play cricket with a bat carved from coconut husk, and he laughs a laugh which Denise is convinced comes from heaven.

Every time Denise hears Perry laugh, she stops what she is doing and sighs: "Lawd a massey. De Lawd wondaful, sure wondaful." Her entire face lights up. Often, she runs to him, enfolds him in her arms and kisses him all over his face, head and neck.

Denise's children don't resent Perry for taking up most of their mother's time and affection. They seem quite pleased that their clinging mother has someone to dote on. Besides, they find their cousin Perry as magical and as adorable as their mother does, not to mention the entire community. Every evening, the children bring Perry four of his favorite snowball sweets on their way from school. On Saturdays, they buy him peanuts and sno-cone, and on Sundays, they use their own money to buy him a royal-chokomo ice-cream, while they settle for a mere ice-sicle or ice-cream stick. Whenever the children go to fairs, they always bring Perry back their "grab-bag" prizes. They feel sorry that he can't go swimming naked in the canal as they do, bird shooting or throwing sticks at alligators down at the swamp. The children regret that he doesn't go to school with them, especially that they can't play pranks together on the way home. They don't understand why he wears an undershirt when it is so hot, or why he is always so quiet and still. Yet they love him. Whenever he gets an especially bad attack, they do their best to be as quiet as they can, and take turns reading to him from their schoolbooks. "Little Will" is Perry's favorite story. Whenever one of the children reads that story to him, his breathing becomes even, his lips curl up and joy lights up his face like a campfire flame.

The big event at Monstrance happens in June when parents dust off their children and send them west, further into the depths of rural life. The reasoning behind this migration is to give the children exposure to true country life—bathing in the river, using a pit toilet and so on. . . .

All of Denise's children, with the exception of the last set of twins and Perry, are bussed to the country to pass the summer with their grandparents. Perry is much stronger and looks healthier, although his legs and arms still look like drumsticks and he still wears his flannel undershirt. However, now he is able to play in the dirt with the twins without getting an attack. Most of the day since the other children have been away, Denise sits and watches Perry play with the twins, her eyes gleaming like a deranged person's. One Thursday she passes the entire day with Perry and the twins, teaching them to play marbles, waddling on her knees in the dirt. And so Dennis finds them at five-thirty—dirty, no pot on the stove.

At the end of summer, Perry is quite well and ready for school. Several times Denise has had to send him to the store to purchase a few items. Always she has written a note listing the needed items, instructing Perry to hand note and money to the shopkeeper. One day, Denise is not feeling well, so she simply tells Perry what to buy and to her utter surprise, he returns promptly with all the items and the correct change. From then on, she doesn't write any more notes and Perry always returns quickly with everything.

Denise still warms Perry's water, but now she only gives him a bath in the evenings. Still, he thrives. The end of August approaches, and the other children return from their grandparents rude and fat. Perry, delighted, runs to greet them. He jumps up and down and claps his hands without getting an attack! His cousins are surprised to see him so active. He plays marbles and cricket with the boys, and he skips rope and plays doll-house (games in which he is always the baby) with the girls. Everyone rejoices, but still Denise watches Perry apprehensively. Whenever the men see Perry on the street, they reach into their pockets and offer him pennies in their open palms. Other children, though older, are only given halfpennies. The women lift Perry up to their bosoms and spin around till both are dizzy, then send him running happily away with a fruit. To all, Perry is a combination of the lost sheep found and the resurrection of Lazarus, so they celebrate his improvement.

School begins in two weeks and Dennis discusses this with his wife. "Nicey, yuh kyan keep Perry to yuh-self faeva" he begins, clearing his throat. "De boy grown into im pants now. Time im guh school, well time." Denise is reluctant. She consults her best friend and advisor Miss Bridget, Miss Paulette, the pastor's wife, and Miss Deborah, the midwife of Monstrance.

The women congregate in Denise's backyard under the large eucalyptus tree. These mothers sit on stools passing a large jar of limeade around. They all know why they are assembled. Their good friend and neighbor has lost her head over a seven-year-old ackee seed-eyed boy. Miss Deborah, who is known for saying exactly what is on her mind, begins before the women are comfortably seated, even before they have had their first sip of limeade.

"Denise, chile, ah know de feelins yuh did feel fah de little man, but yuh behavior gone too far. Yuh put down Dennis an all nine picknie dem an tek up wid Perry. Now, ah did pull out five of de nine heads out yuh womb, suh ah feel ah ave seh in de matta. Ah agree wid Dennis. Perry mus guh school two weeks time."

Miss Deborah takes a sip of her drink and rubs her hands together as if there are crumbs on them. The other women turn in their stools and run their big toes through the dirt. Denise is silent; however, her eyes twitch.

"De Almighty Fada seh 'Thou shalt have no other God but me.' Denise, yuh mus memba dat God is a jealous God. Yuh tek Perry as yuh God. But careful, careful," warns Miss Paulette, refilling her glass to the rim.

The breeze rustles the leaves, sweeping the fragrance of eucalyptus into their midst. Miss Bridget swallows, then spits. She uses the side of her slipper to heap dirt over her phlegm.

The women's thoughts and feelings settle in their stomachs, the way most other things do. Bridget sees the other women looking at her sideways, knowing that they are waiting for her to say her piece. She is nervous, understanding Denise's feeling, knowing how her dear friend always longed for someone like Perry in her life. Yet Dennis and the other women are correct. Denise has made Perry her bosom buddy. Slowly, Bridget runs the back of her hand across her mouth.

"Denise, me is yuh best friend. Me know wha Perry mean to yuh but ah did ovahear im tellin me Joseph how im lookin foward fi start school wid de oda chilren come Septemba. Ah believe if yuh keep im home wid yuh, im wouldn love yuh as much as im duh now. Ah do believe de little angel min well set on being like de oda chilren dem. But let yuh own heart decide, an memba wha we all seh to yuh." As always, Bridget knows exactly the right words to say.

Deborah and Paulette are pleased. The women drain their glasses and enjoy the feel of the breeze.

Picking up a piece of twig, Denise doodles in the dirt. They wait. "Is nuh seh me nuh wan Perry fi guh school wid de rest of de picknie dem. But school is four miles walk. Perry nuh use to walk dat distance. If im get tired or get an attack, de picknie dem nuh know wha fi duh. Oonuh talk true. Me keep Perry as me own special love."

Bridget puts her arms around Denise's shoulder. The women rock themselves back and forth. Separately, each envies Denise, who finds ways to take care of her needs while their desires get thwarted daily by children and husbands.

The wind continues to blow. The women, their thighs spread so that their dresses fall between their legs, sit until the screams and shouts of their children and their empty pots pull them back home.

Denise goes to White Marl Primary School and speaks at length with Miss Wilson, the headmistress. Mrs. Taylor, who will be Perry's teacher, is brought into the discussion and attempts to reassure Denise.

"Don't worry, Mrs. MacFarlane," begins Mrs. Taylor, patting Denise's hand. "Perry will be well taken care of in my classroom. I will place him right up front where I can always keep an alert eye on him. Your older son Trevor speaks very affectionately of Perry, so I feel I already know him."

Denise squeezes Mrs. Taylor's hand. "Ah know Perry gwane like yuh. Im is a little gladioli. Same way im need care like a petal. Love im an im will become as mahogany," Denise ends, with soft eyes shifting from Mrs. Taylor to Miss Wilson.

"Mrs. MacFarlane," starts Miss Wilson in an authoritative voice, "the school will be informed about Perry's health. Mrs. Taylor is one of my best teachers. Rest assured that Perry will not be given any lashes. Although Mrs. Taylor believes, as we all do, that a little whacking helps to lead a child straight, she merely uses her ruler as a threat, rather than as a tool." Denise shakes the teachers' hands and walks down the grading on which the school is perched.

Sunday evening before the first day of school, Perry is put to bed at seven P.M. "Sleep well, me little man," instructs Denise, kissing Perry's eyes and tucking the sheet around him. "Tomorrow is big day fah yuh." Perry reaches up his slender hand and caresses his aunt's cheek, who kisses his hand, quickly turning off the light to hide her tears.

Even though the rest of the children are awakened at six-thirty, Denise wakes Perry at seven Monday morning and dresses him in starched khaki long pants and shirt. He is the only boy, other than his oldest cousin Trevor, who is wearing long pants. His white t-shirt gleams in contrast to his khaki uniform and dark skin. Denise spoon feeds him oatmeal porridge, served with a slice of bread and a glass of milk.

The children wait for him by the gate. "Perry, come me ride yuh to school," offers his uncle Dennis. Perry shakes his head like a chicken whose neck has been wrung. "Nuh, Uncle Dennis. Ah walkin wid de odas. Mama Denise seh ah can walk," ends Perry with pleading eyes.

Denise nods to Perry, then calls Trevor and Linda to her. "Treva, Linda, ah wan both a yuh keep close watch on Perry."

"Cross me heart an hope to die, Mama," declares Trevor. "Ah will tek de best care of Perry. If im look tired, ah will give im piggy-back. Me nah mek a soul boda im. Promise."

Denise kisses her oldest child on the forehead, remembering how he used to squeeze her breast with his tiny hands while she nursed him. The memory makes her blush purple. She turns to her daughter. "Linda, yuh fi hold Perry hand an walk close to im. Nuh boda rush im an race fi be de fus one at school. Memba dat Perry get all stifle up if im run too much."

"Mama, nuh worry," responds Linda, somewhat annoyed at her mother for telling her to do what she has been doing for the last four years with her younger siblings. "Ah will let Perry walk on de bankin. Im won walk in any car an not a soul will touch a stran of im hair." Linda knits up her brow and looks her mother straight in her eyes. Denise, thinking it has been a long time since she has talked with her oldest daughter, takes Linda's hands in hers, holds them for a while and then lets them drop.

It is seven-thirty. The children leave to make it on time for the first bell, which sounds at nine o'clock. Already the sun is bright. Denise kisses Perry on both his cheeks while she merely touches the shoulders of her other children. Dennis shakes his hand and opens the gate for him while she stands by the fence watching Perry, tears trickling down her cheeks. Her husband embraces her briefly before hurrying away, late for work.

The entire population of Bottom Side Lane is out of their houses waving to Perry. The women, their heads tied, lean on their gates and greet Perry as he moves past them.

"Marnin, Missa Perry."

"Tek it easy, little Missa Perry."

"Walk good, Perry, me boy."

"Tek yuh time, Perry, boy, we love yuh."

And so, ushered all the way like Queen Elizabeth

on a momentous visit, Perry begins his first day of school. Tutu, the grandfather of Monstrance who walks with the children until they get to White Marl Road, the main street leading out of Perry's community, is the last person to wish Perry well. The old man reaches into his pocket with bent, bony fingers and comes up with a shiny penny to give Perry.

"Yuh ave a good year a dat school now, Massa Perry, ave a good year." So saying, the old grandfather turns around, heading back for Monstrance.

At school, in general assembly, Perry sits on the platform between Miss Wilson and Mrs. Hall, the deputy headmistress. After prayer, Miss Wilson makes Perry stand on his chair. She addresses the student body: "I want you all to listen and weigh my words well. This lovely child's name is Perry. Today is his first day at White Marl Primary School. I have told Perry that only the best children come here. Remember that. Now let's sing." Tentatively, the students start the school song.

Mrs. Taylor seats Perry between Jennifer and Beverly in the center aisle, directly facing her desk. The two girls giggle and try to nudge each other behind Perry's back. Perry rocks forward and backward, enjoying the new game, until Mrs. Taylor summons him to her desk. She points to a shape:

"Dat's a square, an dat's a circle, an de one wid tree side is a triangle an de one dere wid de two long an two short side is a rectangle. Ah know all me shape dem," boasts Perry, smiling into Mrs. Taylor's face. "Me cousin Trevor teach me." "I see you are a smart boy," encourages Mrs. Taylor, patting Perry on his shoulder.

He scrambles onto her lap. Mrs. Taylor is startled by his easy affection. For the thirteen years she has been at White Marl School, she has never allowed substitute mothering in her classroom, but he does not give her time to collect herself.

"Yuh wan ear me count all de way to a hundred?" Perry spits out each number as if he were competing in a race. When he gets to a hundred, he takes a deep breath, then sings the alphabet. Mrs. Taylor swallows deeply. She had been led to believe that Perry was completely ignorant as a result of his illness. She probes further: "Perry, here are eight different color cloths. Can you tell me what colors they are?"

"Red, black, green, yellow, blue, white, pink an brown. Yuh wearin a blue skirt," announces Perry, turning towards Mrs. Taylor. "Is blue, but not like dis blue cloth. De cloth is lite blue an fi yuh skirt is dark, dark blue. Me Mama Denise have dark, dark, dark blue dress."

"My skirt is navy blue, Perry, and you are right about it being a dark, dark blue."

All morning, Perry sits on Mrs. Taylor's lap while she quizzes him. He tells her that his Mama Denise says he is a bringer of news because he was born January 1, 1956. He talks a great deal, often about his aunt Denise. Before Perry is sent back to his seat between Jennifer and Beverly, he moves his face close to Mrs. Taylor's, causing their breaths to mingle.

"Mama Denise is me bes, bes love, an yuh is me nex bes." Perry jumps off Mrs. Taylor's lap. She runs her hands over her arms and turns to the board.

He prints his name on his paper. His letters are small. The other children continue writing. He looks at Jennifer's paper. She is writing her last name. He scratches his head. His Mama Denise is Denise MacFarlane, but his mother in England is Shirley Thomas. Tears swell in Perry's eyes. Mrs. Taylor comes over and prints "Thomas" on a separate sheet of paper. He rubs his eyes, smiles up at her and prints "Thomas" on his paper.

The end of the first day, Mrs. Taylor walks Perry to the school gate and waves to him as he leaves with Trevor. "Make sure you are here tomorrow, Perry."

Other children stand around and stare at Mrs. Taylor, whispering. The childless forty-year-old widow stumbles. She remembers the first time she met Mr. Taylor. It was the same way—she had been unable to walk as he had stared at her back. She takes refuge in Miss Wilson's office.

"He is adorable."

"And who might that be?" inquires Miss Wilson, still busy with her papers.

"Perry Thomas, of course," glows Mrs. Taylor. "His eyes are deep like the ocean—and such velvet skin. When he smiles, his lips curl up. He has memorized one plus one all the way to ten plus ten, and he recognizes several words by sight and he knows 'Little Will' from beginning to end. I think I have fallen in love with him."

Miss Wilson takes off her glasses and gives her friend a penetrating look. "You love him. Well, so does his aunt, and from what I gather, so does an entire community. Besides, whatever happened to your policy that a teacher should never get emotionally involved with her students? Did that get blown out in one day by the appearance of Perry Thomas? I shudder to think what else will be tossed out the window tomorrow."

At Bottom Side Lane, Denise has burned her hand twice on the stove. She neglected to make her bed until twelve-thirty, when Dennis came home to see how she was coping, and Miss Bridget has observed her sweeping by the gate and looking down the lane at least five times that day.

Denise listens to part of the three-thirty news, her feet itching. She pulls on a clean dress and hollers to her friend Bridget as she rushes by her gate: "Peter and Patsy comin roun back. Watch dem a soon come." Denise trots down the lane, perspiration trickling down her arms.

After walking a mile, she sees the navy blue and white tunics of the girls and the khaki pants and shirts of the boys. She jogs, her eyes scanning the children. Perry is walking at Linda's heels, in conversation with Joseph, Bridget's son. "Eh! Look like Miss Denise runnin to us," shouts Joseph, pointing ahead. Perry drops his book bag and his small feet raise the dust on the gravel road. Aunt and nephew collide into each other's arms. Denise lifts Perry to her bosom and kisses him all over his face. The other children catch up, greet her and continue on their way. She carries Perry in her arms, listening intently as he tells her about Mrs. Taylor and his two new friends Jennifer and Beverly. All the way home, they talk intimately of the day's events.

Soon, Denise adjusts to Perry's going to school, although many days she sits under the eucalyptus tree for long periods, reliving the first few months with Perry. After a few weeks of Perry's absence, Peter and Patsy, her youngest twins, demand more of her time, so she teaches them songs and nursery rhymes.

Mrs. Taylor grows more enchanted by Perry. She sends Denise a letter:

> Dear Mrs. MacFarlane,
>
> I can understand your deep love for Perry. He has become the sunflower in my room. I look forward to seeing him every morning.
>
> Perry is quite eager. He is learning to read and he finds arithmetic very challenging. You have done a wonderful job with him. He is a well-behaved, neat boy. Everyone loves him. In fact, Perry is rather magical.
>
> I would be pleased to have him for at least a day over the Christmas vacation. I do hope you will feel up to sharing the little gem with me.
>
> Most sincerely,
> Mrs. N. Taylor

Perry is nicknamed teacher's pet. William, the bully of Form 2A, corners him in the bathroom: "Teacha pet, kyan get upset, sit pan her lap, oh, oh baby teacha pet." Perry surprises William with a bloody nose and to add insult to injury, William is sent home for the remainder of the day. Jennifer and Beverly kiss Perry, remembering how William always pulled their ribbons.

With the appearance of poinsettias, the first school term ends, Perry receiving a glowing report card. The only thing he needs to work on is kissing the girls less. Denise writes Shirley, Perry's mother, telling her how well he is doing, enclosing a picture of herself and Perry. Shirley replies, enclosing a picture of herself in a fox jacket, and speaks of taking Perry sometime next year to live with her. Denise rips up the picture, flushes it down the toilet, and goes to Bridget with Shirley's letter.

"Now tell me, Bridget, if dis sista a mine nuh damn bad-min? She neba wan spen energy fi love de little man well, but now dat me give me entire soul-case fah im health, she talk bout tekin im. Well, she betta stay in Englan wid she fox coat. Ova me dead body Perry leabe me—Englan too cold."

Perry celebrates his eighth birthday. Denise kills a goat for the occasion and over forty children attend, singing, shouting, climbing and dancing until 10:00 P.M. Mrs. Taylor gives him a toy truck and his aunt dances only with him and Trevor.

Soon, Perry begins to fill out his clothes, and his pants are now short. Every morning on his way to school, he stops in the bushes at the end of Bottom Side Lane, takes off his undershirt, then Trevor helps him to rebutton and tuck his khaki shirt in his pants. One evening before reaching home, he forgets to put his t-shirt back on and his aunt notices. Denise shouts at Trevor, Linda and the other children: "Oonuh wicked suh. Ruinin Perry's health. Lawd mek picknie so deaf ears."

Perry laughs softly at his aunt and embraces her. "Mama, Love," he insists, "de days dem hot, hot bad. De unda shirt mek me sweat like hog." Denise laughs at this but threatens Perry that the first time she hears him coughing he will be back in the t-shirt. He informs her that ever since the new school term began, he has been taking off his undershirt just around the corner from home. Denise pouts, turning her back on Perry, but glances over her shoulder at him, laughter in her eyes.

As the year progresses, Perry becomes more assertive, finds his own friends and often takes a different path home. "Perry, Perry!" shouts Linda. "Yuh betta wait fah me. Yuh know how mama fuss ova yuh."

"Lawd, Linda man," cuts in Trevor, her brother, "mek Perry be im own person. Im nuh baby nuh more who walk in front a car. What Mama nuh know won worry her." Then, turning to Perry, Trevor shouts,

"Perry, yuh jus careful. Wait fah we by de lane."

Perry throws Trevor a smile and runs ahead. Linda sighs and resumes her conversation with her girlfriend; Trevor whistles, his hand in his pocket—he is a man. Sometimes, Perry walks ahead of his cousins, stopping to wait at Bottom Side Lane until they arrive before going home. Sometimes, his cousins have to wait for him, but they do this because they all know that Denise will fuss, thinking it highly dangerous for Perry to walk home without their constant vigilance.

Dennis encourages his nephew's independence and so permits Perry and the other children to go on an outing fifteen miles away. Denise accuses her husband of interfering in matters that don't concern him and initiates a shouting match. "All yuh know do is boast bout yuh picknie dem. Yuh neba boast bout me who bear de pain."

Dennis is silent, weighing his words carefully before testing his wife: "People seh yuh tek Perry fah yuh man bove me."

She rolls her fist and boxes him in the face. Reaching for her hands, he holds them to her back; they struggle, with only the sound of their breathing between them. Denise kicks Dennis off balance. He falls, bringing her to the floor with him, her breast brushing against his chest. Smelling his sweat, she whines, and he cups her cheeks and pulls her mouth to his. Denise frees a hand and rips his shirt open; they roll on the living-room floor, panting.

Dennis still insists on making his point: "Nicey, neglect bad, but nuh bad as drown-wata-love. Yuh ave ten picknie an me is de only husband yuh ave. If me boast bout me picknie dem, is cause yuh nuh tek nuh interes in dem afta dem decide dem separate from yuh. Yuh kyan possess eberyting yuh love or yuh gwane lose de love. Yuh mus gain measurement wid Perry."

Denise buries her head in her husband's chest, wanting only to feel his strength.

Perry's mother continues to write, inquiring about his health, but each time, Denise carefully avoids the questions, implying to her sister that Perry may not after all be doing as well as she previously mentioned.

The end of the school year approaches. Perry is especially happy because Denise has agreed that he can go to the country with his cousins for at least two weeks. All Perry thinks of is swimming naked in the river and going bird shooting. With arms outstretched he spins around, shouting "Mama Denise is de bes, bes person in de whole wide world. De bes, bes person."

Very early, on an exceedingly hot Friday morning exactly two weeks before school closes for the summer, Perry, in a cold sweat, screams out; his aunt, awaking, rushes to his bed while his uncle turns on his stomach and snores. Perry hugs Denise tightly, surprising her with his strength. Gently she rocks him and inquires: "Wha de matta, Perry, me baby, me little man, wha wrong? Hush. Tell Mama. Eh will mek yuh feel betta." For a long time, Perry holds her but says nothing, his tears hot on her shoulder till her own eyes fill with tears.

Quietly, as everyone is still asleep, she pulls herself up with Perry clinging to her neck. Throwing a sheet over him, she creeps through the dining-room door that leads to the veranda. With Perry still gripping her, Denise walks to the rear of the backyard and squats by the breadfruit tree with Perry cradled in her arms. To quiet her own mounting anxiety, she sings:

> Yuh is mine me is yours
> Nuh cry, nuh cry, nuh cry me poo chile
> Nuh cry, nuh cry, nuh cry me poo chile
> Me gwane be here always til nite . . .

Over and over, Denise sings until Perry is calm. "Mama Denise," comes Perry's small voice at last. His voice has the same lifeless ring it had two years ago. Frightened, Denise uses the back of her hand to rub her eye before kissing Perry's cheeks. "Wha me little man wan?" Denise coos. "Me little man know whaever im wan, im will get. Tell Mama." Denise hardly breathes.

"Mama, me dream me turn buttafly an fly far way. Me couldn fine me way back an me neba see yuh again. Me neba see anyone again, Mama, not even yuh."

Denise's tears flow, her head pounds and her heart hammers against Perry's shivering body. She doesn't understand his dream, but she does not like what it suggests, fearful there's something in it she does not want to know. Pondering, she rubs her lips, but emits no happy sound from her throat. She tastes blood in her mouth, swallows, then begins: "A dat worry me little man suh. Perry, baby, yuh can neba guh anywhe whe me kyan fin yuh. Mama Denise will always fin yuh."

Perry smiles a faint smile up at his aunt, cuddles his head against her breasts and goes to sleep. Denise wants to offer him her breast to give them both comfort, but refrains.

Morning breaks with them still sleeping against the breadfruit tree. Birds chirp, roosters crow, dogs bark, and Denise awakes. Perry is curled in the fetal position. She carries him back to his bed and stands looking down at him; then she kisses his forehead before going to make breakfast. Dennis, awake, follows her, a puzzled look on his face.

Twice Denise burns herself. She runs to her bedroom door and peeps in on Perry, afraid to leave him alone—why, she isn't sure. She will keep him home today so they can spend time in each other's company.

She hears her children making their usual morning noises and hollers at them to be quiet. They continue, not heeding her. "Ah seh me nuh wan ear nuh noise. If oonuh wan breakfas fi guh school, shet up." For a while there is silence, but then the children start up again. She stamps her foot in disgust.

After a while, Denise senses someone's presence, and turning her eyes, sees Perry, who is examining her queerly. She feels the heat between them and wants to go and take him in her arms, but is transfixed. "Mama, yuh always wuk suh hard," says Perry, looking out the window and way beyond. Denise smiles but does not respond. "Mama, Love, one day yuh fi stop and sit awhile, but yuh nuh fi cry too long. Jus wash yuh foot in de river." Denise puts her hands to her cheeks; she stares at Perry when he turns and walks from the kitchen, leaving her with sweaty palms.

At the breakfast table, Perry is dressed for school. "Ah was thinkin of lettin yuh stay home wid me today, Perry," Denise stammers, looking at her hands. "No, Mama, ah ave fi guh school, cause today we do de play fah de whole school. No, Mama. Ah gwane school." With a worried heart, Denise bids Perry good-bye, having walked with him for over a quarter of a mile holding his hand and patting his head. Before she turns for home, she pulls Trevor and Linda close to her: "Treva, ah wan yuh fi keep a eye on Perry. Im nuh sleep well las nite. Please, Treva, me nuh bein fussy."

Trevor puts his arm around his mother: "Nuh worry, Mama. Ah will mek sure Perry walk side me all de way to school, but memba dat ah stayin back dis evenin fah cricket practice. Ah will mek sure Linda walk wid Perry." Trevor ignores the jeers from his age group as he walks with Perry, their clasped hands swinging freely. "Perry, a gwane teach yuh fi catch crayfish when we guh granma in a few weeks," offers Trevor, "an we gwane guh bird shootin." Perry looks up at Trevor with large, glowing eyes.

At school, Perry moves from one seat to the next, flitting about like a butterfly. He kisses all the girls, who giggle, interrupting Mrs. Taylor in her lesson. At lunch, Perry goes into Miss Wilson's office and eats lunch on her lap. In the bathroom, Perry tells a classmate that if he pees too often, his teapot will drop off, causing the boy to howl while Perry giggles, clasping and unclasping his hands. Before the school bell stops ringing, Perry kisses Mrs. Taylor and bids her "Mek sure yuh ave a good, good weekend, Miss T."

At Bottom Side Lane, Denise has had the jitters all day. She burns the meat she is cooking for dinner, spanks her twins because they do not come the first time she calls for them, argues with Bridget and neglects to feed the fowls.

On the schoolfield, Trevor is playing cricket with the older boys as Perry passes and hollers at him, "Bat a six, Trev." He throws Trevor a kiss. "Perry, walk by Linda," urges Trevor, throwing a kiss back, which causes laughter among the boys on the field.

Perry walks a few yards in front of Linda and her girlfriends, whistling like a bird while his hands reach out to feel the air currents from the zooming cars. "Perry," calls Linda, "Min! Walk more ova pon de bankin."

Honking of horns and screeching of tires disturb Linda, who turns to her friend: "Lawd, Patsy, dere is suh much noise. Traffic heavy dis evenin. Eberybode a rush fi get to market."

"Gal, all dese moto cars mek me fraid," replies Patsy. "Me glad seh jus up de way we tun off dis main road." The children walk on, Perry ahead, skipping and whistling. Then a car swerves in and out, misses Linda and her friend, but lifts Perry off his feet. He lands on the car's fender, then rolls off under the tire of an oncoming truck. A split second.

Denise holds her head and screams, feeling as if her head has split open. "Wen me Perry get home, ah will feel betta, ah know ah will feel betta. Im should be comin soon."

The car that knocked Perry off his feet and sent his body into the air has crashed into a light-post. The door jams and the driver, his forehead bleeding, tries to get out, another passenger trapped inside.

Perry's body is sprawled in the street, his hands flattened into the tar, his head a mess of blood and bones and white runny matter on the asphalt.

An explosion. People scatter, running for cover. The car that hit Perry is ablaze, its driver and passenger trapped within.

Linda screams and runs ahead, staring. She tries to make out the once smooth black body of Perry, but her eyes meet only blood, flesh and guts. She remembers that time she saw the butcher Mr. Henry casually slit the goat's neck and watch the blood trickle into a pan. With the same indifference, Mr. Henry cut open the goat's stomach, causing its warm, still pulsing intestines to spill out. Linda tried to swallow but she vomited, and for a week she could not keep anything solid down, and gave up eating blood pudding. Now, seeing the remains of Perry, Linda feels her stomach revolving but nothing comes up. Only her mouth tastes like vinegar and onion. She remembers her mother's warning: "Linda, ah wan yuh fi mek Perry walk by yuh an hole im hand." Falling to her knees, Linda rocks to and fro, sobbing "Lawd, Mama gwane kill me now, Mama gwane kill me."

A crowd gathers. The women sigh and half shield their eyes, the men stare ahead and spit, children jump from one leg to another, some putting their thumbs in their mouths. There is no conversation; only a mumbling issues from the group. A woman goes over and puts her arms around Linda, who screams louder: "Mama gwane kill me, Lawd, Mama gwane kill me. Perry kyan dead!" People move from one foot to the other, not going anywhere. Time passes. A flock of blackbirds flies overhead westward, and just then the ambulance arrives. The ambulance attendants screw up their faces hard and take deep, slow breaths. The drunken-driving weekend ritual has begun early.

Heading home are Trevor and his friends. "Hey, look—people dem, mus accident" one boy offers, sprinting ahead. The ambulance speeds off just as Trevor spots Linda and goes over to her. He doesn't understand a word she says, but he knows instinctively what happened and his stomach turns. He bends over. He is the oldest and therefore responsible.

Voices from the crowd address him: "Shame how dat drunken man kill off de little boy!"

"Me nuh know why people mus be in mad rush come Friday evenin."

"De little boy was way ova pon de bankin; mus drunk de man did drunk, but see, God tek de murderer in fire."

Trevor wipes his eyes with his shirt collar. Perry threw him a kiss as he left school and his friends laughed at him when he returned Perry's kiss. He was going to teach Perry to fish. Confused, Trevor takes off in the direction of the ambulance.

At Bottom Side Lane, Denise has made up Perry's cot more than eight times. Finally, she lies down on it, feeling very tired. "Me little Perry rite: me wuk too hard." Rising, she shifts from one foot to the other. "But wait—it gettin late, 5:30; Perry dem should be ere. Well, is Friday. Dem mus stop fi play wid dem friends."

Misses Bridget and Deborah, returning from the market, talk about going to see the new school play next week in which Perry is cast as the village chief. Noticing the drifting crowd, Miss Deborah asks a passer-by what happened. "One drunken man run ova a little boy—kill him flat dead," comes the response, followed by a gust of spit. Miss Bridget sees Linda and the other children and learns that Perry has just been run over—killed. She hugs Miss Deborah and they cry, tears staining their faces. Bridget cries out: "Oh, Massa God! Sometimes yuh act cold, mitey cold!"

Deborah breaks in, "Little Perry did jus begin look good. Im jus start full out im clothes an laugh a belly laugh like eberybode else. Lawd, im jus begin mek im aunty feel like er love did pay off."

"Yes," cuts in Bridget, "Lawd, Massa God, de little boy bring we such pleasure. Mek you mus tek all de best fruit, wha mek?"

"Hush, Sista Bridget, hush. Is nuh fi we place fi question de Lawd. Im gi an im tek way."

Denise gets up, turns off the radio. 6:00 o'clock. She sighs: "Whe de picknie dem deh? Poor me Perry mus tired bad." She mopes around the kitchen, trying to prepare an easy meal for her family, but her head feels heavy and it aches, so she swallows two Phensic to alleviate the pain and ties her head.

Misses Bridget and Deborah put aside their tears, embrace Linda and lead her between them. The other children walk behind, stupefied. The questioning is endless: "Why Perry? Im neba fight nor quarrel with nuhone. Im always pleasant an quiet."

By the time Misses Bridget and Deborah, Linda and the children reach Bottom Side Lane, Perry's death has been recounted several times and twenty other people from the community have joined them, sharing their tears, fear and general feeling of loss.

Denise is getting ready to go and meet Perry and the children when she hears the noise at her front gate and goes to investigate. Seeing the children, she smiles, her eyes scanning them for Perry. "Whe me man deh? Perry, whe you hidin?" Suddenly she becomes aware of the mood, and notices Linda's tear-stained face. Mother and daughter look at each other.

A woman in the rear of the group shouts "Denise, chile, Perry gone from us, gone like de wind."

Linda cries out: "Mama, please, a nuh me fault. Perry did walk ahead, an de car come from nuhwhe. Please, Mama, ah beg yuh is nuh me fault; please, Mama, ah love Perry, too."

Denise turns her back to the crowd, her head moving from side to side like a broken branch dangling after the hurricane. The tears and comments grow silent while Denise relives her last moments with Perry earlier this morning. Perry knew—he had tried to tell her, to prepare her. Denise reaches out and touches Perry's imaginary face—his gleaming skin, glossy eyes, languid body. This morning, she had wanted him to suck her breast and all day she had thought about that desire to share some part of herself with him. Now, he wasn't there to share it with. "Yuh nuh guh know how me titty well sweet, Perry."

Turning back to face her children and the crowd, Denise sees Linda through clearer eyes. Acknowledging the remarkable child she has, she embraces her, pulling Linda to her bosom and rocking her. Then, turning to the group, she raises her hand to silence the crowd. Misses Bridget and Deborah move forward to put their hands around Denise, but she wards them off with a brush of her hand, and putting her children behind her, she closes her gate. A woman places her hand on her head and sings "He lives! He lives forever more!"

"Hallelujah. Let it be said," Denise declares, addressing the crowd, "Perry live; im was a little angel sent ere fi sit wid us a while." She resonantly declares: "Lawd know Perry did full me life, till me own flesh didn't exist until after im satisfied. Ah worship de little man. Im live alrite, an ah gwane weep an mourn fah im now de Lawd tek im way. De Lawd wan fi look pan Perry pretty face." Denise's voice begins to crack. "Lawd seh im lend me Perry long enough. Well, ah guh weep an mourn till ah tumble down." Denise looks up towards the heavens, and her face reflects the expressionless silver-blue vault.

People mumble to themselves and each other. A man shouts: "Let eh out, Sista Denise! Cry till yuh tumble down. Let eh out."

"Nite fallin, suh let we turn in." Denise turns towards her house.

Dennis, having heard of Perry's death at work and rushing home, encounters the crowd at his gate and passes through it to stand by Denise. He is proud of her strength, but knows all her energy will falter as soon as the dead is buried and the final dust is put in place. He embraces her and she throws her arms around his neck, pulling him close to her. Smelling his sweat, Denise remembers that Saturday morning they fought about her self-indulgence over Perry. He holds her firmer and she thinks that from now on, he will always have to hold her like this.

The crowd departs slowly, heads low. A tear wets Dennis's shirt. It is much too soon, she thinks. On the veranda, Denise turns around: "People, oonuh guh home. Men an chilren wait dem supper. Oonuh guh home an attend to life. Me family wait me an de dead still need im good-byes. Gwane an wait till Monday; oonuh come wid oonuh tears an lament to praise de dead."

She enters her house with her man beside her and her children at her heels. From this moment, she often refers to Perry as "Me Man Angel." His name is placed in a box to be given to someone special.

After their eight children have been fed, and

though Trevor is still missing after his flight from the scene of Perry's death, Denise and Dennis prepare to go identify Perry's body and make preparations for the funeral.

The night is hot. Dennis carries Denise on the bar of his bicycle. The sky is silver and indigo blue, with a half moon. He pedals slowly, his thoughts on Perry, who used to sit curled by his feet like a puppy— Perry, who never got into any mischief, and who was always grateful for any small gift. "Yes, suh," slips from Dennis's mouth, "Ah did truly, truly love dat boy. Dere was somtin peaceful bout im. Yes, suh, somtin quiet like de river in de late evenin."

They reach the hospital and are directed to the morgue, which is at the extreme rear of the hospital, nestled between trees. A porter leads the way. Nearing the entrance, they hear a voice wailing "Perry, Perry, Perry," and turning, they find Trevor crouched under a tree.

Denise bends and kisses away her son's tears. "Mama," comes Trevor's faltering voice, "im jus kill Perry fi nutten, Mama, fi nutten im kill Perry. Me spit in im face, Mama."

Denise holds Trevor in her arms. "Son, sometimes we nuh undastan so we hit out. We ave fi accept sometimes, accept even though eh hard. Me an yuh did love Perry bad. Lawd knows me soul-case jus like de sea at storm."

The porter shuffles his feet. Dennis helps up Trevor and Denise and they turn to follow the porter. Inside, the tray is pulled open. Perry is not there. Only mutilated meat. Denise swallows, but still it comes up and comes up,and the weary ache that she has been carrying around all day in her stomach and head goes. She leans against the wall while Dennis helps the porter clean up her spew. After taking some deep breaths she turns to Dennis: "Leave me, leave me wid Me Man Angel, leave me." Dennis isn't sure she'll hold up, but the porter leaves willingly.

Alone, she turns to the tray and sees Perry still dressed in his school clothes. His left shoe is missing, but he still wears his navy blue socks and long khaki pants. His shirt has become a part of his body—red and crushed in.

His matty hair is covered with red and white matter, his jaw is twisted, and his eyes are open in a smile. She gazes into Perry's eyes and hears his voice for sure saying "Mama—Love yuh fi stop an sit awhile, but yuh nuh fi cry too long." She reaches into the tray and caresses the remains of Perry's face, then rubs her numbed fingers together, feeling a film of ashes on them. Feeling a hand on her shoulder, she turns and smiles at her husband and son: "Perry open im eye an smile wid me." She looks from Trevor to Dennis, her eyes dancing. Dennis nods his head in agreement: "Yes, Nicey, Perry always smile at yuh."

The three walk the seven miles home from the morgue, Dennis pushing his bicycle all the way. She looks in on her children, who are snoring. A few are near the edge of their beds, but Linda is wide awake. Touching Linda's hot forehead, Denise is startled at the difference between her temperature and Perry's. Denise rubs Linda's body with bay rum and puts her in Perry's bed to sleep.

Man and wife sit on the front veranda, rocking until way into the early morning. As they get up to go to bed, Denise turns to her husband and asks, "Den, Perry eye did open wen de porta pull out de tray?" Dennis scratches his head. He doesn't know—isn't sure—so he shrugs. Denise, leading the way to their bedroom, muses, "It nuh matta. Dem did open, den dem close."

Before dawn has properly broken, Miss Bridget comes, bringing food for Denise and her family. Shortly, Miss Deborah and Miss Paulette arrive. The three women take over, dividing Denise's children among themselves while Dennis goes to send Perry's mother a telegram.

Left alone, Denise goes back to her bedroom and undresses as for birth. She lights a white candle and anoints her body with olive oil, spending time to massage her joints, working her hands as if she were doing

Perry's body. Then she lies on Perry's cot and falls asleep. Dennis awakes her at 9:30, presenting her with a cup of tea and a slice of bread. At first, she is confused. It is night. She slept the entire day. In the same manner, she passes Sunday, having only another cup of tea.

Monday morning, she rises before the rooster has announced the day and goes to her backyard by the breadfruit tree, where she suckles Perry.

The first workday of the week finds the Monstrance community frantic. White shirts have to be found and starched and black dresses have to be darned or loosened. The MacFarlane house is scrubbed from top to bottom and a huge pot of curried goat and fish soup is cooked to serve all the people who will come after Perry's funeral. Denise takes great care to dress her three daughters in their white Easter Sunday dresses and white patent leather shoes sent to them by their Aunt Shirley in England. All her boys, except for Trevor who has on a grey suit, wear their khaki school pants with white shirts. As Denise looks at her children, she is suddenly filled with admiration. She murmurs, "Oonuh guh wid Miss Bridget to de church. Leave de house suh me can dress."

Denise looks around at her house, quiet for the first time all day. She throws up her hands, realizing that soon people will invade every corner like a marching band of ants. As she sits on the stool by her dresser, her face stares back at her from the mirror. She reaches up and touches her tightly drawn skin that she has not looked at in more than a year. Her life has been too busy with children and domestic chores, time only to take a bath and pull on a dress. She smiles at her reflection, liking her face. She is surprised at the softness of her hair. Over and over, she brushes it, forgetting the gathering crowd at the church, anxious in the late afternoon heat. Finally, she stops playing with her hair, pulls it back tight in a bun, turns to put on her black dress, but throws it to the floor. It is an ugly dress with its mournful seams. Searching through her closet, she takes out her yellow dress that she had worn to her youngest twins' christening, remembering how

Perry had complimented her: "Mama, dat's de mos prettiest dress. Yuh look jus like a sunflowa."

"Yes, me little angel did like dis dress. Me gwane wear it an spit pan anyone who seh me sin fi nuh wear de tradition."

People are crowded by the three doors of the church. Half of the seated congregation are schoolchildren in uniforms. Denise enters the church from the rear and walks up the aisle like a bride, stately, holding her back stiff and her head high, a secretive smile playing on her face. As she advances, the church grows quiet except for occasional whispers. She smiles at the congregation, tempted to laugh at their conventional expectations, but she refrains, knowing that they will only think that she has lost her head. Besides, they don't know that Perry wants her to wear yellow and look pretty with make-up on her face. Mrs. Taylor gives her hand a light squeeze as she passes by her bench. Denise slowly takes her place in the front row with her husband and children.

The pastor immediately begins: "Let's rise. De Lawd giveth an de Lawd taketh away, blessed be His name. Let's sing 'Gentle Jesas Meek an Mild.'"

The congregation struggles to rise, gasping like an old locomotive. Voices fill the air:

> Gentle Jesas meek an mile
> Look upon a little chile
> Pity my simplicity
> Suffer me to come to thee . . .

At the end of the first verse, Denise flops on the bench and closes her eyes, too tired to act as expected. She does not wish to hear any more about sinners, forgiveness, repentance or any of the other words and phrases which have nothing to do with her life, and certainly not Perry's life or death. Before long, she dozes.

She is shaken by her shoulder just as the pastor is asking for the lid on the coffin to be sealed. She rises, goes up to Perry's coffin, looks down at that face etched with calm, kisses her fingers to her lips and then places them on Perry's cold forehead. She looks up at the congregation, who are waiting to see her cry, falling to the floor in grief so she has to be carried from the church wailing. She is again tempted to let them have the show, but Perry was her own and she refuses to share him. She looks again at Perry lying in the coffin. He smiles up at her, and she waves to him and walks out of the church.

It seems a long time before the crowd files out of the house of the Lord. Perry's coffin is placed on a buggy drawn by two brown horses. She climbs up in the buggy and sits beside the driver while her husband and children walk behind, the host of schoolchildren, Mrs. Taylor and Miss Wilson following, with the community bringing up the rear. The three miles from the church to the graveyard take well over two hours, the procession singing all the way.

At the gravesite, the pastor begins: "The Lord hear thee in the day of trouble, the name of God . . ." Denise does not wish to hear any more religious song or scripture. All afternoon, her soul has been drowning, until now it seems like the washed-up skeleton of a fish. Perry doesn't understand any of these songs or words. Denise wants to experience Perry's going as a special event, not as a simple funeral with a spool of dirges. She pulls up her body, and her spirit rises forth and soars. "Stop all dese songs wid de ready-made grief. Fi me time fi sing an tell Me Little Man Angel bye."

Silence. The people pull in their arms, hugging themselves. Denise instructs the diggers to lower the coffin. As Perry's body descends slowly, she sings the nonsense song she made up and sang to Perry the morning before he died:

> Nuh cry, nuh cry, nuh cry me poo chile.
> You is mine an me is yours
> Nuh cry, nuh cry, nuh cry me poo chile
> Me gwane be here all day till nite.

She cups her hand with dirt and throws it on Perry's coffin. The crowd follows and the grave is filled.

Denise parts her way through the crowd and walks home by herself, Linda following at an appreciable distance. A crowd has formed in her yard and the people keep coming until they extend to her gate. Food is passed around, groups form and the conversations are all in favor of Perry. She listens to the chatter and sucks in her tears like a newly dug hole absorbing water. After a while, no longer able to bear the touches and words of condolence, she walks to the backyard and sits under the breadfruit tree. "No, sah, Perry will neba die, neba die."

A shadow. She looks up into her husband's face. He pulls her up, embraces her and she is suddenly glad that he's so sure of her love and so silent in his ways. They walk back to the house. The people are all gone and her children are still with her friends, so she and Dennis undress by the candle's glow. "Tomorrow ah gwane visit wid me moda. De river will do me good." She faces Dennis.

"Good, yuh need de change. Treva an Linda well responsible fi tek care de younga ones. An Bridget always jus ova de fence." Dennis gets in the bed and Denise lies down beside him. He enfolds her, but she tosses and finally throws his arms from around her. They are quiet. She gets up and goes and lies down on Perry's bed.

He snuggles up to her. Denise pulls her knees in, lying like a chair on its side. They comfort each other, mother and child. She sleeps soundly, wakened at 11:00 A.M. by the constant bark of a dog.

Denise opens the window and peers through it. She sees her children surrounding Tutu, the grandfather of Monstrance. He has a puppy in his arms. She pulls on a dress and goes to her backyard.

"Well, daughta Denise, ah see yuh decide fi face de day. Little Perry been up since six."

Dennis and his children look down at their feet. They believe Tutu does not understand Denise's grief because he is so old.

"An wha yuh bring from Perry, Tutu?" inquires Denise calmly.

"Dis ere frisky barkin pup fah yuh picknie dem."

"Ah tank yuh, Tutu. We did need somtin from Perry."

The old man bows to Denise, turns and leaves. Denise looks at the wiggly Dalmatian.

"Yes, Lawd, dat's from Perry, alrite. Is man dog. We mus call im Perry-Face." So saying, Denise picks up the puppy and cuddles it.

· Widows' Walk ·

SHE goes looking for Neville. This is obvious to all. Many times she has to blink her eyes, which keep fooling her into believing that she sees his boat out at sea. It is only a mirage. Another wave swells up before breaking on the shore.

June-Plum was tense all week, even before Neville left, but she never articulated her fears. Then, just before he left Sunday morning, she broke a saucer —a sure sign of unpleasant news. She didn't know then that it was connected to Neville, but she should have. Several times within the last couple of weeks she was visited in her dreams by a beautiful chocolate-colored woman with thick, wild hair piled upon her head like a straw basket. This shapely chocolate goddess with inviting hips and thighs wore a cloud-white dress with several ruffles of blue cotton that flounced with her every move. She taunted June-Plum that she was the more desirable of the two, but June-Plum did not heed. She stubbornly refused to believe that her dreams or the broken saucer might have anything to do with the very contented life she led with Neville. How foolish could she be? June-Plum bursts out with a big laugh of astonishment at her own foolishness.

June-Plum's deep belly laughter, so big that it scared people off because they couldn't imagine a pleasure as enormous as the one her voice suggested, used to delight her mother. "Yuh gi weh laugh fi peasoup," she would say. June-Plum recalls that her laughter was like peasoup in those days, in neverending supply. Happy memories of her mother heighten June-Plum's sadness and she fixes her face like a funeral mask. She lingers on the boardwalk long after all the other women have turned into their houses and closed their windows to bar the mosquitoes entrance. A handful of stars shines through the purple sky. To block out the wind, June-Plum folds her hands over her belly swollen with child. The waves are just ripples gliding calmly, and, at each fold, they glitter. There is almost no flow, only motion going nowhere. The effect is inviting, yet disturbing.

Neville should have returned yesterday. The smell of smoke and burning bush (to keep the mosquitoes at bay) swirls through the air like perfume—no, more like the pungent smell of the flamboyant tree's blossoms. June-Plum sighs and hugs herself more tightly, hearing the waves beginning to grumble.

She searches the expanse of water while waves splash against the boards, sending salty foam rising up like vapor into the night. Each time she thinks she sees something, someone. Who is this goddess Yemoja? As ruler of the sea and children, she is as generous in her gifts of children as she is ruthless in taking men. But June-Plum is not her enemy. She, too, is woman and mother, and she wants her man. This one Yemoja cannot have, and June-Plum means for her to know this, means to challenge and fight her if need be. As her thoughts take form, June-Plum takes in a deep breath and lets it out with a sigh. She takes several abortive steps before throwing off her slippers and descending into the water to wet her feet.

The waves rush in as if to meet her challenge. They chase her and she runs to and fro before standing her ground, lifting her dress until her thighs are bared, confronting her competitor with knowledge that she too has thighs, almond-stained and diaper-soft, which wrap themselves around her man's back when he enters her deeply, pleasing her to tears. But soon June-Plum is disarmed by the comforting touches of this woman. She eases in completely, and the salty water, cool, bathes her aching heart and massages her weary limbs so that she forgets herself and simply imagines Neville's hands about her body as the waves continue to recede.

Gasping for breath and swallowing water, June-Plum treads until her fingers touch the sandy bottom.

She wipes salty water from her eyes, shakes her head and drags her drenched body to the shore, sighing and laughing. This woman is mistress indeed, and more powerful than she, June-Plum, could ever hope to be. Flopping on the damp sand, she wonders where the sea ends and the sky begins, as it all just seems a mass of blue and white foam. But it doesn't matter; she likes the unity of blues—only how can she and Neville become melted in unity like that? Then she remembers that Neville is already part of that unity. The woman has already taken him. He might be that very wave which is the same as the one before and no different from the one which follows it. June-Plum knows that she could not win if she fought Yemoja, so that all that is left is pleading, hoping that as a woman Yemoja will understand her need and give her back her man. "De sea so pretty; yuh so free an easy. Ah ave fi gi Neville time wid yuh, but memba dat me need im."

June-Plum comes to the quay and strolls along the boardwalk, the sea mewling beneath. Her sense of destiny tells her nothing. What is today, anyway—Wednesday? Thursday? Friday? Yes, it's Thursday—Thursday is the only day the fishermen sell their fish to whoever comes to buy, not putting aside any for the higglers, the small vendors. Neville left early Sunday morning, when the sky was ashen white and the wind oblique.

"Im been gwane longer dan tree days before. Why me mus worry meself wid bad expectations?"

"Nite, Miss June-Plum, yuh out ere late by yuhself."

"Bertram, ah didn't even ear yuh approach."

"Yuh nuh fi worry yuhself. Ah confident widin me body Neville gwane return safe."

June-Plum allows herself to hear what Bertram has said. He is confident Neville is safe and will return. She doesn't know if she should laugh at such consolation. She is doubtful . . . afraid . . . not able to eat anything. Not sure of what to say, she looks up at the sky. "De nite so pretty. Not often de sky so purple wid stars. De sea calm. Look how de waves hardly move.

De book people dem seh de world round, den somewhe at de hedge de sea an de sky lock fingers."

She looks out at the sea, forgetting that Bertram is with her. Her mind cannot hold any one image; it flits from Neville to the children, to last Sunday's sermon, to all the wash that still has to be done. Why is she here on this walk? Her children are home asleep and she should be in bed. And her husband is at sea or gone. June-Plum rubs her arms where cold-bumps have appeared, then turns, remembering Bertram.

"Bertram, wha yuh doin out ere? De nite wind cold. De sky an eberyone lie wrap warmly in bed. Yuh ave a good nite an seh howdy to Beverly."

She lingers longer on the boardwalk, raises her wet dress and examines her thighs. Then, on impulse, she pulls off her dress and jumps into the sea, floating on her back like a piece of log washed to shore. She probably would have passed the night there, but she is suddenly aroused by a harsh voice and firm hands that drag her out of the water and roughly pull her dress over her head.

"Is fool-fool yuh fool or is nuh sense yuh ave. Ooman, yuh ave picknie in yuh belly an four at yuh house—is mad? Yuh mad? Way afta midnite yuh a wade in de sea. Seems like yuh nuh know de sea bad. She nuh joke; she is a funny ooman. Seems like yuh mus mad." And so Miss Country, the old woman who sells fried fish, roast fish and bammy from a little shack by the seashore, reprimands June-Plum as if she were a disobedient child. At this, June-Plum laughs and allows herself to be pulled along and fussed over by Miss Country, who walks her directly to her house and makes sure she is safely inside.

At home, June-Plum makes herself a cup of cocoa and the radio provides company while she rambles around the kitchen wiping off clean counter tops and drying plates that are already stacked in the cabinet. Finally, she sits and folds her hands in her lap. A couple of times she catches herself nodding. . . . "Who on de ladder? Neville, wha yuh doin up dere? Eberytin look so funny. De sea upside down! Whe all dis leaf come from on dis wata-wooden shack? Neville, min yuh drop! De ladder nah lean pan nutten! Wata can't hold yuh. Mek de sea so rough. Neville, come down, come down, de ladder a shake. De waves gwane cova yuh!"

June-Plum focuses her eyes and looks around the kitchen. Her cup is half full of cocoa and the only sound that comes from the radio is hissing. She didn't hear the national anthem but she knows it is after midnight, so she pulls herself up heavily from the chair. Four children have made her stout and motherly, and in another four months, there will be a fifth. She doesn't want any more children as times are too hard, but the pill is something new, unfamiliar, and Neville never will use rubbers. She sighs. The Bible did say be fruitful and multiply. She hangs her dress on the nail behind the door and opens her Bible:

> Then the Lord said unto Moses, Now shalt thou see what I will to Pharaoh: for with a strong hand shall he let them go, and with a strong hand shall he drive them out of his land . . .

Something bangs. June-Plum springs out of bed and runs to the back door, thinking Neville has returned. Mist and emptiness greet her. She goes outside into the yard, opens her back gate and looks down the lane. She sees a figure. A smile rushes to her face, and her voice is a gong in the night: "Neville! Neville, yuh come home." She waits by the gate, suddenly aware that she's barefoot and in her nightie. The figure disappears and only the night remains. Again, her eyes have deceived her. No, she tricked herself—allowed herself to be fooled.

She closes her gate and looks out at the wailing sea that is sending big waves up to the sky. Then she sees her, the woman with whom she shares her man. Yemoja is riding the waves. A lacy turquoise and white turban is wound around her head, ascending to the sky like a cone. She wears strings of shells around her neck and arms and she is naked except for a satin blue cloth around her waist. This cloth blows in the wind like miniature wings. Yemoja's nails are blue on fingers and toes, and a diamond fills the gap between her front teeth. She is beautiful, more lovely than the moon, more lovely than an idea. June-Plum bows to her. Yemoja winks at her, then dives into the roaring waves.

June-Plum is suddenly very cold. Shivering, she runs into the house, bolting the door behind her. For several minutes she stands by the door afraid to move, trying desperately not to think of anything, not even Neville. After several deep breaths, she walks to her children's room and switches on the light. They are all there—safe. More or less. She shakes her head. The noise she heard was her youngest son Garfield fallen off the bed again. She looks at her children—two single beds, four children, a little dresser, and there is no place to turn in the room. June-Plum sighs, rubs her stomach and bends down—bending tears at her back—and picks up Garfield. She starts putting him back on the bed beside his brother Floyd, but then, she turns and takes him to sleep with her. June-Plum tosses. Garfield kicks her at every turn. A rooster crows one, two, three times. The sun rushes through the window like an unwanted fly. June-Plum pulls her dress over her nightie and heads straight for the kitchen, where she puts on water to boil. She burns herself.

"Jennifa, get up. Wake up yuh broda dem, an come grate de chocolate fi mek oonuh tea."

"Marnin, Mama, me a fi guh school today? Ah could help yuh wash an company yuh to de market."

"Jennifa, nuh boda ask stupidness: Yuh know yuh go to school wen it rain, wen yuh sick, an if school did open pan Saturday and Sunday, yuh would guh too. If me did only ave fi yuh chance."

"Daddy come home today, Mama?" Jennifer cuts off her mother, having heard her mother's lament numerous times about how she had to leave school in the fifth class after her mother took ill to help care for the house and the other children. June-Plum sizes up Jennifer and reaches for the bottle of Solomon Gundy (smoked herring with pepper and escallion), her craving, along with guavas, since she became pregnant. She smiles, thinking if it's a boy she will name him Solomon and if it's a girl, Guava. After all, that was how she got her name, June-Plum. Her mother supposedly ate several of the green prickly plums daily during the last two months of her pregnancy.

"Mama!" It's Jennifer, interrupting her memories: "Daddy comin home today?" June-Plum regards her daughter and is angry at her question. She doesn't know when her husband will return, if he ever will. Since she has to make some response, she snaps, "Yes, Jenniffa, maybe."

That early hour of the morning, the sun shining through the kitchen windows reminds June-Plum of a pack of fierce, charging dogs. She feels the heat very keenly, and her thighs are beginning to sweat and rub against each other. She raises her dress and examines her thighs, another of her habits since being pregnant, and gradually becomes aware of someone watching her. As she raises her head, her eyes meet Jennifer's, who acknowledges her look before turning to the stove. Jennifer's eyes are so like her missing father's that June-Plum kisses her teeth before emitting one of her deep belly laughs as she leaves the kitchen and walks to her backyard. From there she surveys the sea and the entire community. In another couple of months it would have been ten years since she and Neville began living here where the sea and its smell are always dominant.

Anton Bay is a fishing community. The sea is everywhere. The dock has been christened "Widows' Walk" because many wives, sweethearts and mothers have paced the boardwalk awaiting their men, some of whom have returned from fishing trips while others have not. Women usually gather there in the evenings to exchange gossip, to throw kisses to their men already out at sea and to stare and marvel at this beautiful/ treacherous woman who feeds them, lulls their men and soothes their bodies with her waters. Mostly, though, the women wait. June-Plum feels as if she's been waiting all her life like the rest of them for a man to bring happiness into her life.

This morning, the sea is a smooth blue blanket in sharp contrast to her backyard, which is a mixture of gravel and leaves. The guava tree is in bloom, but birds have picked at the green fleshy fruits. June-Plum runs her hand between her thighs, waves a nonchalant hello to someone passing by her gate, then goes and sits at the open kitchen door where swarms of flies compete, and where a few minutes later her children stumble past her, after kissing her on the cheeks, on their way to school.

June-Plum settles in the doorway, her back partially resting against the door frame. She pulls up her dress and absent-mindedly massages her thighs as she again succumbs to her memories.

Ten people were living in four small rooms and she was one of the ten, the older of two girls and the fourth of eight children. When she was eleven, her mother had a stroke, so she had to leave school to wash khaki pants, darn plaid shirts, clean wooden floors using a coconut husk, cook, and on occasions, help dig yams and pick cocoa to sell at the market. The work was not as painful as not being able to go to school, and the Bible was the only book in the house to read. So each day, June-Plum would read to her mother. She began at Genesis: "In the beginning God created the heaven and the earth. And the earth was without form, and void; and darkness . . ."

Halfway through Revelations, her mother died. "And there was given me a reed like unto a rod; and the angel stood, saying, Rise and measure the temple of God. . . ."

June-Plum didn't cry at her mother's death. Nor at the funeral, and not even during the Ni-Night celebration, the feast for the dead nine days later. She was happy she didn't have to live each day with the painful look in her mother's eyes and so she grew, keeping things to herself and surviving without friends. She learned to be patient and to cup her sadness in her palms—to guard her feelings.

For ten long years, June-Plum washed clothes, cooked and cared for the house of her father and brothers, while Jennifer, her sister, had been rescued to live with their maternal aunt and family. Jennifer had not come home to visit, but she always remembered to send June-Plum a card on her birthday. And that was why June-Plum named her first daughter Jennifer—in remembrance of her sister.

June-Plum rouses herself. The children's breakfast dishes are still on the table. She looks at them and frowns, moving off into the room where she and Neville have slept for the last nine years. She sees Neville curled up on the bed, covered from head to foot, regardless of the heat. She tugs at the sheets and he dissolves right in front of her eyes. . . . A wail rocks her body. Her lying eyes.

In a drawer to the back, hidden under some clothes, is a picture of a man and a woman. The woman is slim and tall, wearing a white dress that stops midway between her knees and ankles, a white hat, and white shoes. In her hand is a bunch of hibiscus flowers. The man is tall and muscular, wearing grey baggy pants, a white shirt and plaid bow-tie. His face says his shoes are pinching his toes. The woman's smile does not conceal the uncertainty she feels about herself, but they look nice together, standing beside a bicycle which the man holds. June-Plum sees only the bond that exists between the two persons as she recalls how she met Neville.

On her way from the market she had stopped to buy fish, as her father insisted on having fish for dinner every Saturday. Neville had been riding his bicycle, shouting: "Fish! Fish! Fresh fish! Fish nice wid yam, fish nice wid rice, fish an bammy, fish an chocho, fish an pumpkin. Fresh fish! Buy some fish!"

She waved him down and watched as he jumped off his bicycle with ease, reached into his back pocket for a handkerchief and wiped the sweat from his face before looking at her and flashing her a mischievous smile.

"Wha de lady wan fi buy?"

"Leh me see yuh snapper."

"De finest snapper yuh gwane get, mam, de very finest. Catch dese meself early dis marnin."

"Yuh fisherman, too?"

"Yes, mam. Catch me own fish an do me own sellin."

June-Plum resented him calling her mam, especially since heat was prickling between her thighs. She barked at him, "Gi me five pound snapper."

"Yuh wan me clean dem, mam?"

"Nuh worry, me'll clean dem meself."

"Yuh husban an chilren gwane enjoy dese fish."

"Me nuh ave no husban, nor chilren sah."

"Such a pretty ooman like yuh."

"Yuh sell fish out ere ebery Saturday?"

"Yes, mam."

"Good. If me like yuh fish, me will look out fi yuh." With that, June-Plum walked off, feeling the fishvendor's eyes following her. The thought made her stumble, so she was glad when she moved out of his vision and only his voice was heard trailing off in the distance: Fish! Fish, fish, fresh fish. Fish nice wid yam, fish nice . . ."

June-Plum shakes her head at those memories and goes to sit under the guava tree. From there the sun moves from directly above at noontime to an angular slant indicating that the day is passing, but still June-Plum sits, the memories traveling through her head until she is startled when Blackie her dog barks and runs off to greet the children returning from school.

Floyd is the first to approach: "Mama, is true Daddy lost at sea?"

June-Plum's heart skips a beat and she makes laughter drown her fear. "Floyd, mek yuh mus ask stupidness, go inside and tek off yuh school clothes." The children all go in to be fed.

After dinner, the kitchen clean, June-Plum moves to her veranda to pass the evening in her cane rocker. Every so often, she is interrupted by a good evening or a howdy or by the children's bickering, but for the most part, her mind lingers in the past.

The next week when she went to the market after she hurriedly bought yams, tomatoes and other produce, she sought the fishman. When she heard "fish,

fish" behind her, she turned around with delight on her face, but only a toothless man with greying hair hopped off his bicycle, coming to stop in front of her. June-Plum looked at him, kissing her teeth before walking away. She had not run into the young fishman. Disappointed, she climbed into the bus and slumped down on the seat. There was no fish in her basket. A woman carrying two large baskets entered the bus and accidentally brushed against her, and June-Plum immediately flew into a rage: "Yuh did gi me dress putdown. Yuh tink me is wall fi push gainst!" All of her pent-up anger and frustration were released. Two older women sitting in the back of the bus commented quietly that John Crow must have spat in June-Plum's eyes, while another woman, looking pleased with herself, declared that all June-Plum needed was a good piece to keep her quiet. At this, the men in the bus chuckled and massaged their crotches, while the bus sped around corners at a dangerous speed, sending goats, chickens and people scampering onto the bankings.

When June-Plum got home, her father greeted her: "Me did sit ere worry bout yuh. Yuh out late."

"Me a big ooman an can come an go as me please," she retorted.

"Chile, wha troublin yuh? Wha mek yuh vex wid de whole world?"

"Me jus tired," complained June-Plum. "Me nuh clean an cook an keep house fi nobody but meself nuh more."

The next day, June-Plum quietly packed an old cardboard suitcase and left home, heading for an unknown destination with very little money. After numerous failed attempts at securing a job in several towns, June-Plum went to a bus stop to rest. The sideman of one of the buses bounced off his bus, picked up her suitcase and secured it on the top carriage of the bus.

"Come, daughta, jump in; we ave fi keep movin."

She complied and the bus lurched off, sending her stumbling down its aisle. At the next town, Anton Bay, thirty-six miles away, she got off. The town was surrounded by the sea. The air smelled salty-sweet.

Four fishermen with nets were gathered, talking. June-Plum walked past them, glancing at their faces, hoping to see the young fisherman. They nodded their heads and bid her good evening. Timidly, she reciprocated the head gesture. Her feet were tired, but she must find a job and somewhere to sleep. She came to a small grocery store and entered.

"Mam, could ah trouble yuh fah a little ice-wata?"

The woman behind the counter looked at June-Plum from head to toe before going to the back of the store from where she returned shortly with a glass of water. June-Plum drank thirstily. Finishing, she wiped her mouth with the back of her hand.

"Tank yuh, mam. Me did well thirsty. God bless yuh." She moved off to go, and still the woman behind the counter had not said a word. June-Plum turned to her: "Excuse me, mam, ah new ere. Know anyone who wan help?"

"Yuh can count money?"

"Count money? Yes, mam."

"Yuh know how fi handle people?"

"Yes, mam, me had to deal wid me eight broda dem."

"Yuh start now?"

"Start, mam?"

"Yuh wan de work or not?"

"Yes, mam, but . . ."

"Yuh a fi live in, keep yuh room clean, help keep de shop clean an sell behine dis counter ere."

"Yes, mam."

"Yuh in de family way?"

"Oh, no, mam, me nuh sleep wid man yet."

And this was how June-Plum and Neville finally got together. Two weeks after June-Plum began working in the shop, the fish vendor rode up and parked his bicycle in front of the shop. A happy mood came with him.

"Pretty daughta, whe do ooman?"

June-Plum looked at him and was tongue-tied. He did not remember her, at least so she thought.

"Daughta," he began again, his eyes shining, "ah wan yuh fi tell de ooman dat de fishman out ere wid her favorite fish."

At that very moment, the woman walked in and the fish vendor turned to speak to her, leaving June-Plum to stare at him. The woman and the fishman were on good terms, joking with each other. When the woman took the fish and went to the back of the shop, the fishman turned to speak to June-Plum: "So how yuh like workin wid de old ooman? She nuh talk much, but she is a good soul."

He laughed as he spoke, but June-Plum just stood there. He ordered a soda which he took his time drinking, relishing each swallow. June-Plum turned her back and began straightening the jars of sweets, sweat forming on her brows and beneath her armpits.

The fishman watched her, remembering the first time he saw her.

June-Plum remained with her back to him, her heart racing.

"Daughta." It was the fishman. "A little youth wan buy sometin."

June-Plum turned and attended to the little boy while the fishman finished his soda. She then took his empty bottle and went to place it in the crate with the other bottles. When she turned back to face the counter, he was already on his bicycle, shouting, "Fish, fresh fish, fish nice wid yam. Fish nice fried, fish nice fi mek soup, fish . . ." His voice trailed away. For the remainder of the day, June-Plum pouted and was short and unfriendly with all the customers.

It was several weeks again before June-Plum saw the fishman and it was only then that she learned his name. He entered the shop and his presence was like a welcome afternoon breeze. "Wha happen, pretty daughta? Long time nuh see. People who know me call me Neville. De old ooman seh yuh call yuhself June-Plum. Me like de fruit well bad and me like the person who guh by de name, too."

Neville reached over as if to tickle her and she drew back, startled. "Who vex yuh suh? From dat first

105

time yuh buy snapper from me, me did wonder who step pan yuh toe. Yuh fi laugh. It will do yuh good. Yuh name suit yuh: yuh fleshy an nice an prickly, too."

So June-Plum smiled because she felt happy and because Neville the fishman was jolly, and yes, her name told of her personality.

They became friends, and each week when he came, she had his favorite soda ready for him and they talked and laughed and he told her when he would be coming again. For four months, Neville and June-Plum only saw each other inside the shop. Then, on one of his visits, he asked her to go to the dance with him.

At the dance, Neville was popular. His friends shouted greetings and June-Plum, shy, did not know how to act. Neville sensed this, so he kept his arms around her. A pretty woman with pearly teeth came up to Neville and stroked his arm, and June-Plum felt her face get hot. She wanted to slap this woman, to stake claim. The music was loud and sensuous, but she did not feel confident enough to dance. Neville insisted, though, so they danced, June-Plum losing herself in the rhythm and heat of the crowd. After a while, Neville took her outside, where it was cool, and kissed her on the mouth. She felt hot and faint. It was her first kiss. She pulled away from him and ran ahead. Neville caught up with her and she abandoned herself to him, resting her head on his shoulder.

Six months later, during the hurricane season and the dark nights, June-Plum, two months pregnant, moved into Neville's one room and two months later one Saturday morning, they dressed up and went and got married. It was the first time June-Plum had had her picture taken.

"Mama, Mama!" It is Floyd, shaking her gently.

June-Plum wonders if she is dreaming. "Neville . . . Neville is yuh? Yuh come home?"

"Mama, is nite an Daddy nuh come yet. Time yuh guh bed." Floyd is embarrassed by his mother's tears. He helps her off the rocker, locks the door behind them and leads her like a blind person to her room. As he walks back to his room, he mumbles to himself:

"Me hope Daddy come tomorrow. Im gwane longa dan im seh."

June-Plum tosses and wakes at every turn. She's afraid to sleep, visualizing herself swallowed up by the sea. She's angry at Neville for not coming home and not sending word to her. She hears her heart racing and tries to drown out the noise by covering her chest with Neville's pillow. This only adds to her agitation, as she smells Neville until his smell fills the room. June-Plum pants for breath. Neville's smell and the sea's—his face and Yemoja's—merge, making her dizzy. The bed spins and June-Plum holds on for dear life. The splashing of the waves rises to a crescendo and all she can do to keep from going mad is to hold her head and plead, "Please, please, leave me alone. Yuh can keep Neville. Keep im." After a while all noises stop and June-Plum dozes, waking at 5:00 A.M. She gets up and heads for the beach, where the fishermen are drawing in their nets. The early morning air is cool and the grey of the night is almost gone. On the beach, she abandons her slippers and heads towards the group of fishermen. She makes out Tony, Bill, Bigger and Nobel—no sign of Neville. Still, she approaches the men, whose muscles are taut from hauling in their nets. Bigger is the first to notice her:

"Marnin, June-Plum. Neville still out pan de sea?"

"Seems like it, Bigger. De sea is im true wife."

Well, yuh know we men ave fi ave more dan one wife."

"Wha mek? Guess we oomen just ave fi catch who catch can."

The men turn back to their fish and nets. June-Plum stands looking at the fishermen, a forlorn look in her eyes. As the sun begins to peep over the horizon, she walks further down the beach where the rocks jut out forming a closure, and there, she undresses and wading out into the water, submerges her body all the way to her neck. Her teeth chatter and she can feel cold-bumps all over her. By the time she comes out, the fishermen have gone off with their haul and only a tangled net and fish bones are on the beach. June-Plum bends down and scoops up a handful of sand which she sends swirling through the air, crying out Neville's name at the same time. She does this three times, then scoops up a handful of sea water and drinks it. She is beginning to understand Yemoja, more powerful than any person, including herself. She is a force in nature that prevails. Surrendering to her is not defeat; it's wisdom. June-Plum breathes more easily as she heads home.

Her children are already at the table eating breakfast. She is grateful for her very independent children. She kisses them all on the tops of their heads and sits where a place is already set for her.

"Mama." It is Garfield, her youngest. "Daddy come?"

"No."

"Wen im comin?"

"Soon."

"Mama," cuts in Jennifer, "how Daddy gone so long?"

Floyd comments, "Im seh im would be back Wednesday nite. Today Friday."

"Me know wha day it is, Floyd," June-Plum offers weakly.

"So wen Daddy comin?" insists Jennifer.

"Oonuh guh to school an stop de one million question."

"Mama, yuh tired?" As usual, Dawn, her very sensitive daughter, is concerned. June-Plum shakes her head in denial. Four pairs of eyes stare at her; she stares back at them, massages her thighs, sighs, and then declares, "Oonuh Daddy comin soon. Now guh to school fore oonuh late."

The children scramble out and June-Plum follows them outside, stopping by the guava tree where she squats for an inordinately long time before going back into the kitchen. She turns on the radio just as the announcer is saying, "It's 10:45 this beautiful Friday morning." The morning is passing. June-Plum looks around her kitchen. The dishes are still there from breakfast, there are clothes to be washed, the house has to be cleaned, and there is still much more to be done. She goes to fetch the dirty clothes. At the door, the sun blinds her and she shields her eyes. Blackie, by the fence, sees her and comes and rubs up against her leg. When she bends and pats his head, some of the dirty clothes fall to the ground. June-Plum looks at Blackie and smiles. He is her only company all day and she is in the habit of speaking to him.

"Blackie, whe Neville, deh? Ah time im come home. Me nuh like man who stay out longa dan dem seh."

Blackie whines in response and June-Plum rubs his back. She puts the clothes in the basin to soak, and goes inside to wash the dishes and to prepare lunch for Dawn and Garfield, her two younger children. She takes a long time doing everything, and by the time she finishes cleaning the kitchen, Dawn and Garfield are home and she has not made lunch for them. She sends Dawn to the shop to buy four patties and two cocoabread, which they have with mango nectar.

Afterwards, she walks her children back to school, all the while looking behind her, craning her neck out to sea, looking for a familiar sight. June-Plum stands by the school fence watching the children play. In all of their movements, she sees Neville with his strong arms pulling in his net full of fish. After a while, when the bell has rung and all the children have gone to their classes, June-Plum wonders why she is there. She does not want to go home and wash clothes or finish her cleaning. She resolves to wander until her feet decide where they will lead her. After all, genius is a capacity for withstanding trouble.

Finding herself at the seashore where some boys about ten years old are swimming and playing naked in the water, she looks at them, examining their small bodies, black and wet, glistening in the sun. She remembers, it seems like for the first time, how she used to swim naked in the river with her sister and friends before her mother died. But that seems like another life. Remembering that scares her. She had forgotten all the good times before her mother died. Could she so easily forget Neville? Since her marriage and four children, her body has become stout and, yes, ugly—something to be covered up. She throws off her slippers and pulls up her dress. The water is warm and the sea is very different today—not so blue, and seemingly satiated. The boys see her and cover their privates. June-Plum bursts out laughing and calls to them in a friendly voice.

"Nuh boda cova up. Me ave boys an see tings ebery day."

The boys giggle and continue to splash each other. The water feels so good June-Plum wades in further, wanting to go deeper until it reaches her shoulders and then covers her head. This woman, this Yemoja, is alluring with her blue waters. June-Plum pulls up her dress further, lapping it between her thighs. Two more steps forward and her dress will be up to her panties, but she cannot stop herself. She wades further. Perhaps if she shows Yemoja how capable she is of holding up despite the loss of her man, if she stops competing in a game that she does not understand therefore must lose, then maybe Yemoja will leave her alone to bring forth another life and to enjoy the four she has already been given. Clearly Neville is out of her hands now, completely in Yemoja's power.

"Sista June-Plum, come si down wid an ole ooman an remine er of tings." It is Miss Country, as old as spit. No one in the community knows Miss Country's age, but she seems older than the trees. Everyone who comes to the village sees her, and she knows everyone: children, cousins, aunts, uncles and grandparents, and even great-great-grandparents. Miss Country spanks any children she sees misbehaving and sends them home to their mothers, who come to thank her for caring. Children are almost perfectly behaved when Miss Country is around. She is nutmeg color with a face as lined as the Sahara Desert. Toothless, she seldom smiles. Her arms are strong like a man's and she never wears shoes, her soles rubbery-tough like a tire. She says when she dies they can sell her feet to Bata, the shoe store chain. June-Plum loves Miss Country and is not put off by her roughness. "Come, Sista June-Plum, yuh moda neba tell yuh fi min ole people?" Miss Country walks off, erect, a large basin of fish on her head, her stool in her right hand and a large knife in her left.

June-Plum pulls herself out of the sea and runs to catch up with this living history. Her legs are wet and her dress clings to her thighs, her firm and shapely thighs that she loves. People meeting June-Plum salute her with "Peace" and "God-bless," but no one mentions Neville, though everyone knows. Everyone in the village knows even the most intimate details about everyone else, down to how many times a week a woman "does it" with her man. So June-Plum knows that they know. She feels like a naughty child caught in the act with everyone whispering behind her back.

She sits on an empty crate and helps Miss Country gut her fish and wash them off with lime. Only their eyes and hand movements speak. Two pretty grey-turquoise ground lizards play nearby. Miss Country is smoking a cigarette with the lit part inside her mouth. June-Plum has always wanted to ask Miss Country how she smokes with the fire inside her mouth, but she has never had the nerve. It was the same way she felt around Neville. There was so much she wanted to ask him, especially Sunday morning before he left when they lay awake in each other's arms. She had wanted to ask him how he felt about their having another child, but refrained, fearful of what he might have said. She couldn't bring herself to tell him how much she loved him either, how she wanted then to do something because she didn't want any more children. But her heart was in her mouth and she didn't want to spoil the peace, the beauty of the moment, because she knew—sensed—that Neville would not be returning as he said. How could she have known and not said anything, not done anything, to prevent him from leaving? June-Plum was too accustomed to acquiescing, to waiting patiently like a good woman for her man. Well, those days were over with she decided. From now on, others would wait for her. Neville's going freed her of the cyclic burden handed to her from her mother, who took it from her mother before her. Women forever waiting for something to happen. June-Plum sees Miss Country observing her. "Betta late dan neba," she mumbles to herself and pushes out her chest. She will ask Miss Country about the fire inside her mouth.

"Miss Country, yuh eat de ashes dat fall from de cigarette inside yuh mout?"

Miss Country looks at June-Plum and frowns. "Wha mek a big ooman like yuh mus guh lif up yuh frock, expose yuhself to boy picknie? Neville nuh guh like it wen im come back an people tell im how yuh act foolish."

June-Plum spits. Silence surrounds them like a mosquito net. "Miss Country, yuh tink Neville comin back?"

"Me look like de sea to yuh? Me an dat sea-ooman nuh bosom-buddy, she nuh tell me nuttin."

At this, June-Plum knits her brow but says nothing.

"Wen de baby due? Yuh mus tek advantage of some a de new ways. Yuh an Neville a sensible people. Picknie expensive. Galang a yuh yard, guh cook fah yuh picknie dem."

June-Plum wipes her hands and heads home, feeling admonished. She looks back, and Miss Country is still gutting and cleaning fish with smoke coming through her nose and the lit part of the cigarette hidden inside her mouth. She still does not know how Miss Country is able to smoke without burning her mouth, but she shakes her head and moves on. Just before turning inside her gate, she looks out at the sea and sees Yemoja standing in the center of Neville's boat, combing her hair with a long wooden pic. June-Plum kisses her teeth and turns her back on her rival.

Her children are sitting around the kitchen table, a sad lot, looking like wet puppies. The suhsuh from their friends at school, who, in turn, heard it eaves-dropping on their parents, has is that their father is lost at sea. Floyd and Jennifer are upset by this rumor. They remember that last year one friend's father and uncle drowned during the hurricane season when their boat capsized. Their father was a good swimmer, it wasn't hurricane season and he had painted his boat blue and white in honor of the sea goddess Yemoja, but there were no guarantees. The sad faces of her children assail June-Plum. She silently warms up yesterday's fried fish and rice and puts the food in front of them. Her stern look warns them not to ask any questions. Blackie is fed most of the evening meal. She sends the children to play, but the girls, Jennifer and Dawn, choose to remain with her. They sit on the veranda but all are restless, so June-Plum decides they should go for a walk. They stop every so often to exchange greetings and a few words with people on the street and to clap at the mosquitoes that buzz around them. They end up at Widows' Walk.

June-Plum stops and stares out to sea until the shades of blue make her dizzy. Unsteadily, she holds on to the railing. Miss Country can be seen seated by her tray of fried fish. Jennifer and Dawn are playing closely by the seashore; they have abandoned their shoes and are wetting their feet. June-Plum sees them, but they seem far away. She calls to them, but no sound comes from her mouth. The waves are full. A trail of blackbirds is flying home. The sun is lost in a cloud. She looks at the waves. They dazzle and pull. Her head spins. Her thighs feel like logs. Suddenly she is going down, down. The salty water plays around her face and gets in her ears. She can feel the damp sand beneath her and hears the gentle cry of the waves. This woman means to take her, too, so she succumbs giggling, her mother's words echoing "yuh gi weh laugh fi peasoup. . . ."

June-Plum finds herself lying in bed. Her head swirls like the waves. "Whe Jennifa and Dawn? She tek dem too? Neville seh de sea is im most beautiful ooman; dat why im love er. Im love er more dan me."

113

Miss Country, hearing June-Plum's chatter, enters the room and proceeds to rub her face and neck with bay rum. June-Plum smiles, still thinking she is a part of the sea, and remembers her earlier jealousy— how she wanted to master this woman, this sea which surrounds their lives and is woven into the beauty of the landscape. She is everywhere one looks and her song is the consistent noise lulling one to sleep. Almost all of the men of the community belong to her and sometimes in her greed, she takes one or two of them to live with her permanently.

Neville spent two weeks fixing his boat. He painted it dark blue with light blue oars, and he and Bertram and some of the other fishermen bought a large bottle of white rum to offer to the gods for protection and good luck. In addition, he had Basil, the local artist, draw a stately black woman with big legs and nappy hair like a mane surrounded by foliage at the stern. She was as June-Plum had seen her in her dreams—beautiful, enticing. Neville was so proud of himself he invited the entire community out on the beach for a feast and Miss Country prepared the fish and had everyone licking their fingers and smacking their mouths for days after. With this larger boat Neville could get a bigger haul on each trip. June-Plum was happy for him, but she was never able to say this to him, as each time she felt a lump in her throat.

His net is heavy. The waves are furious and sudden. He smiles, his white teeth the only light in the dark night, his laughter drowned by the wailing of the waves. Neville relaxes and surveys the sea. "Ooman, yuh wild tonite. Yuh mus need more rum." For a moment there is calm. Neville reaches out to pull in his net, but just then, a big wave tosses the boat. He lets go, losing his net. "Wha vex yuh, ooman?

Relax—mek we talk nuh." Another wave comes, and still others. Neville wrestles with his boat, but the waves have pushed it into a current and he is unable to take control. "Now look ere, ooman, me ave wife a yard. She nah guh undastan." Neville is pulled along and the waves cave in on him, creating a valley. He sees no way out. He surrenders to his mistress, Yemoja, who leads him further, taking him into her depths until he goes under, smiling . . .

"Nooooooo!" June-Plum screams, her voice echoing through Miss Country's house and out the window, stopping passers-by in their tracks. Miss Country, in her kitchen listening to the news on her transistor radio sent to her by her great-grandson in New York , hears that a fisherman was found at sea.

Miss Country enters the room again and faces June-Plum, who is sitting up straight as a board, perspiration covering her face. Miss Country chews on her gum and shakes her head at June-Plum. "Radio man seh dem fine a fishman. Yuh should kill dat big ole roosta yuh ave an mark yuhself wid de blood."

June-Plum stares at Miss Country, who apologetically mumbles, "Me neba did hear nuh name. De radioman neba seh nuh name," she ends, staring at June-Plum, who slumps back on the pillow, the child kicking in her stomach. After what seems like an eternity, the thought comes to June-Plum like a whisper: "De beautiful ooman tek him!" Tears fill up her eyes, but she quickly wipes them dry, ashamed of her weakness. Miss Country's eyes relate an understanding of her grief as she hands her a cup of tea. June-Plum drinks the pumpkin leaf tea, then slowly gets out of the bed, Neville's words playing in her head, "bet yuh ah tickle yuh." She hugs herself and bursts into a laugh, an attempt to drown the sob rising in her bosom. The sound is hollow, disconnected, joyless, stopping Miss Country from leaving the room.

Miss Country looks at her: "Chile, yuh a loose yuh head?"

June-Plum shakes her head, her face shining like a full moon. Yemoja was always more woman than her. The sun is bright—splendid, in fact. June-Plum parts the curtains and looks out. Seeing people dressed in their Sunday best, she is confused. It was Friday evening when she went walking with Dawn and Jennifer. Miss Country anticipates her question: "Yes, yuh did sleep an toss an act fool-fool fah a whole day an nite. De picknie dem alrite. Wen yuh faint, Dawn run come get me. Big ooman like yuh should know fi eat wen yuh a carry chile."

Suddenly, there is a great commotion. "Miss Country! June-Plum! June-Plum! Neville alive an comin home, Neville alive!" It is Beverly, Bertram's wife, running and panting with the news. June-Plum sticks her head through the window, her eyes large. Beverly grips her hand. People on their way to church wave to her. June-Plum is immobile for a while. Then, with great haste, she pulls on her dress, leaving her hair wild. Her slippers clap as she hastens to her house, thinking of all she has to do before Neville comes home: wash dishes and clothes, clean, bathe herself and kill that rooster. Beverly says she will help. Neville is alive after all.

As she hurries along, June-Plum feels young again. She remembers that first evening she and Neville went to the dance, his mouth wet and hot on her neck, his arms firm around her waist. People greet her, but her smile is not for them, it is for Neville.

OUR MOST RECENT RELEASES

SIMULACRA
Collaborative work of
monotypes by Kate Delos
poetry by Rena Rosenwasser,
limited edition with 14
full color plates
$23

SMALL SALVATIONS
Poetry and prose poems
by Patricia Dienstfrey
illustrations by Kate Delos,
letterpress edition
$8.00

ORDERING INFORMATION

Individual Orders
Please include payment with order.
Postage & handling is $1.00 for 1-3 books.
Add 15 cents for each additional book.

Bookstores & Libraries
discounts
1-4 books   20%
5-10 books   40%
over 10 books   45%

ORDER FORM

Title	Quantity	Price	Total

Ship to:

Name

Address

City   State   Zip

Send orders to:
Kelsey St. Press
P.O. Box 9235
Berkeley, Ca. 94709